# What the critics are saying...

"Ms. Lapthorne's 'Merc and Her Men' is a sensual exploration of different aspects of sexual and emotional relationships... Be prepared for strong sexual content and have an extinguisher handy because this is one hot story!" ~ *Trang Black, Just Erotic Romance Reviews*

"Merc and Her Men" had my attention glued. I've enjoyed *Ms. Lapthorne's* books before, but the sheer animalistic eroticism in the beginning of this book was different. It was hot!" ~ *Dani Jacquel, Just Erotic Romance Reviews*

5/5 cups "Ms. Lapthorne knows how to write sex scenes that will send the reader to the shower to cool off. The ménage a trois session is one of the hottest I have ever read. In addition to the great sex, the action sequences are exciting and the love story will bring tears to the reader's eyes. ~ *Candy, Coffee Time Romance Reviews*

"Whew! Talk about one hot book that will definitely leave a lasting impression on any reader whose favourite number just happens to be three." ~ *Courtney, Romance Reviews Today*

# Elizabeth LAPTHORNE

Merc
AND HER
MEN

ELLORA'S CAVE
ROMANTICA PUBLISHING

An Ellora's Cave Romantica Publication

www.ellorascave.com

Merc and Her Men

ISBN # 1419952927
ALL RIGHTS RESERVED.
Merc and Her Men Copyright© 2005 Elizabeth Lapthorne
Edited by: Martha Punches
Cover art by: Syneca

Electronic book Publication: May, 2005
Trade paperback Publication: November, 2005

# Warning:

The following material contains graphic sexual content meant for mature readers. *Merc and Her Men* has been rated *E-rotic* by a minimum of three independent reviewers.

Ellora's Cave Publishing offers three levels of Romantica™ reading entertainment: S (S-ensuous), E (E-rotic), and X (X-treme).

*S-ensuous* love scenes are explicit and leave nothing to the imagination.

*E-rotic* love scenes are explicit, leave nothing to the imagination, and are high in volume per the overall word count. In addition, some E-rated titles might contain fantasy material that some readers find objectionable, such as bondage, submission, same sex encounters, forced seductions, etc. E-rated titles are the most graphic titles we carry; it is common, for instance, for an author to use words such as "fucking", "cock", "pussy", etc., within their work of literature.

*X-treme* titles differ from E-rated titles only in plot premise and storyline execution. Unlike E-rated titles, stories designated with the letter X tend to contain controversial subject matter not for the faint of heart.

## Also by Elizabeth Lapthorne:

*Merc and Her Men*

## Author's Note

I have always been intrigued by the fantasy of a threesome. And so, in my usual impulsive fashion, I decided to write a short story about a woman who met up with two old flames and indulged herself. I have to laugh looking back. One thing led to another, and now here I have a full-length book. Something I think we all need to be reminded of, every now and then, is that life so often throws us the strangest twists and turns. Why not enjoy them?

# Chapter One

Kyli sat alone at one of the few small tables scattered throughout the small bar. She felt grateful that it had been placed underneath one of the few dingy light sources, hoping it would make her more visible. She knew the evening ahead would prove to be interesting, not only because she had been sitting here, waiting patiently, in the outlier bar for nearly twenty minutes, but also she was onto her third Blue Vodka.

Not smart for a single woman who wished to remain unmolested. Picking up the shot glass, she made sure her left hand rested as close to her beamer as possible but not be labeled as a threat.

Sure, as of six hours ago she no longer could call herself a merc, but her rejected application from the Force had only arrived in this afternoon's mail. Kyli restrained herself and only took a tiny sip from her shot glass.

*"We regret to inform you that your application to the position of Novice Investigator to the Force was unsuccessful..."*

Kyli cringed at the still crystal-clear memory. For a woman who had happily faced down armed rebels, traveled through space for years on end to secure outlying posts and free slaves, she had been surprised at how badly upset she had felt hearing the cold, unyielding words from the monotonous drone of the rejection-hologram the Force Recruiting Department had sent her.

All new recruits were warned of the dangers of close proximity and the stresses they underwent, both as individuals as well as the entire team. Physical relationships were a hazard on many levels. More than one heartbroken recruit left the wet team, never to return to any segment of the Force again.

Kyli smiled to herself a tad cynically. She had survived not one broken relationship, but two.

Gregor had been her first. Her first in many different respects. Not only had he been the first man for her to sleep with in their wet team, but he had also been the first man for her to share her deepest, darkest fantasies with late at night and often as dawn crept over the horizon.

He had been the first man whom she truly loved, and the first man who had taken her full surrender. Through coaxing and skill he had tempted her beyond reason, tempted her to let him bind her to their bed and pleasure her as none had previously. She had screamed for him many nights, both to continue as well as to stop.

It felt odd to be reminiscing about him and the times they had happily, even eagerly, shared after all these years. She still couldn't label the mix of feelings he had raised inside her. He had taunted her sexually, but in such an erotic, dark manner she hadn't been able to help herself, hadn't been able to stop the roller coaster of lust she had ridden with such abandon.

It had been Gregor who had awakened inside her the love of sexual bondage. Oh, she could happily have a relationship outside the dominant and submissive games. However, she had learned under his erotic training that underneath the sexual being she knew existed, there also lay in wait deep within her heart and body a sexually submissive side of herself.

With the games he played, and they played together, he had blended such an erotic mixture of pleasure and pain, often she didn't even know which she screamed for more of. For the pain, she discovered, enhanced the pleasure. And the pleasure, under his skilful hands, cock and mouth, had easily been the most erotic, powerful feeling she had ever indulged in.

Ever.

She had gloried in his thin golden chain of possession, which she had worn secretly underneath her suit as a constant symbol of his claim. She had loved the lush, decadent thrill of feeling the manacles close over her wrists, knowing he would easily spend hours tasting and touching her body, preparing her for his eventual penetration.

Yes, Gregor had been a first for many things with her. And even though she had loved him, it had been a dark, fleeting sort of love.

As she had grown older and wiser, Kyli had learned many men and women came to love their tutor, to love the person who opened those special doors for them. She had come to realize this dark, forbidden love of hers for Gregor fell into that category. It in no way lessened her feelings for him, yet neither could it be a love one could build a life upon.

Her love for him felt true, but had been skewed by that of student adoration. She had been so grateful to have this new, completely unexplored world open up to her, she had needed him to show her all they could bear. Wrapped up in this tutor/student relationship had been her conviction only he and his mind and body could bring her this pleasure.

She had never felt the same level of passion of dark surrender with anyone else. It had been so very different to any other experience she had that she could never be certain her mind hadn't simply expanded on what had been brilliant bondage sex.

Even though she had loved every lesson, wallowed in the sheer erotic enjoyment, they both had known it would only last a short time. *The student always will move on,* he had whispered to her one night, as they lay entwined in each other's arms after hours of lovemaking.

Even though Kyli had voiced a denial, insisting they would never part, she had heard the catch in her own voice, realized they would, one day, part and go their separate ways.

And so, much like any secret, forbidden set of lovers through the millennium, they had stolen every moment possible. Gregor had used them both well. He had introduced her to spanking, to exotic nipple and clit clamps that could both heat the extremities and send tiny, harmless electric pulses through the system. They had played with vibrators of every shape and size and for every style of play.

Kyli shivered in remembered lust at the times she had shared with Gregor. Even though all the memories with him were happy, erotic thoughts, she knew she would always slightly fear him. For with Gregor, she had cast aside every inhibition. There wasn't anything in the whole known galaxy she hadn't been willing to try with him, or let him do to her.

And in that freedom from her, lay a form of power for him.

A power Gregor had never abused, and thus she always felt safe with him, but the man did hold immense erotic power over almost every woman alive. His eyes, his innate knowledge of women throughout the universe made him a master of sexual prowess. It genuinely felt as if he could read the secrets and desires every woman held. And he was a strong enough, masterful enough man that he could bring all those dreams and desires into reality.

Their relationship had come to a natural though slightly painful conclusion when Gregor had been headhunted by the International Secret Services. In the training camps his encryption and computer skills were legendary and to more than just those who were in the wet team.

Everyone had known of his uncanny skill with the codes and complexities. It hadn't been a surprise to anyone he had been headhunted. The surprise lay in the fact he had still been such a young recruit, barely finished with his preliminary training when he had been secreted away by the ISS.

Even though he had been a year or two older than most of the rest of the team, to be headhunted by the ISS before the end of wet training had proved the high level of his skill.

Finishing her shot, debating the wisdom of whether or not to let loose and move onto her fourth shot, Kyli laughed at herself. She didn't have to worry about whether she had the next shot or not. It wasn't as if she had to get up for work or training the following day.

Besides, she consoled to herself, she had held herself under such rigid control for so many years she deserved at least *one* night of wallowing in self-pity before she picked up the pieces of her fresh new life. Once again she would follow wherever her own whims, and the goddess, would lead her.

Having decided what to do, at least for the rest of tonight, she signaled the scantily clad femserver for another shot of Blue Vodka. Her thoughts, completely of their own volition, returned to Gregor. She remembered how they had both been sad, but not heartbroken, to call an end to their mutual sexual marathons.

Gregor was a good friend, someone she could rely on, but he was firmly placed in her past. Before tonight she hadn't thought of him for years. For a few years after their separation he had left her cryptic and sometimes not-so-cryptic notes on her personal carrying computer, or PCC.

Enjoying the memories, even if they did invoke a bit of the old longing, Kyli looked down to the mini-comm attached to the side of her watch. It had been years since she had received a message from Gregor. She had always assumed he'd been either killed in action or simply too engrossed in his new life to remember his old one.

Not that Kyli thought of him that often either. Returning to old haunts brought up past successes and failures. Thankfully, Gregor fell firmly into the success basket, both as a friend and lover. Heaven knew there were few enough of her lovers scattered around the universe that she still counted as friends.

She didn't know exactly how to contact Gregor, but she knew if one of them ever tried to contact the other she felt certain each would be alerted, and undoubtedly come to help. That knowledge and certainty counted for a hell of a lot in her book.

Kyli thanked the femserver as she left the shot on her table. She'd give her mysterious guest another ten minutes and then she would head on home. She had an unopened bottle of Red Whiskey she could move onto to continue her "celebration". If she was determined to get plastered tonight to forget the fact her life had taken a few wayward turns recently, she might as well do it right. Tomorrow she would begin to plan how to enter the Force.

Looking around the dim bar Kyli tried desperately to ignore the most potent of her old memories.

Frowning, she realized it might just be easier to remember them and then move on. Looking down at the untouched shot, she raised an eyebrow at it and herself.

*Tonight must be the night for remembering the past.*

# Chapter Two

Kyli wrinkled her nose, and much like pulling an adhesive bandage, tried to rip out all the painful memories at once. One after the other, images flashed through her Blue Vodka-numbed brain. It had all begun a month or so after Gregor left. She and Max had been the last two recruits left behind in the bar, laughing and teasing each other to death.

Memories of necking with Max, letting her tongue run over his lightly-stubbled jaw, rushed through her brain. Visions of taunting him with her love-struck blue eyes, and seeing the heat flare inside his own, so *very* dark brown eyes, in response.

Kyli remembered playfully pouting her lips and watching the heat of recognition and sensual promise awaken and burn in his eyes. She knew he would satisfy her, touch and caress her until they both ached with the need for each other.

She remembered spending the minimal amount of time here with the rest of their wet team, and then race back to his lodgings, making fierce love until one or both of them fell into an exhausted sleep. Then when one awoke, they would start all over again until dawn crept over the horizon, forcing them to return to their training.

Max, she couldn't kid herself, had broken her heart when they had split up. She had wanted to enter the Special Armed Forces, just as he had. Yet he had been arrogant enough to not only interfere with her application, but to then ask her to not join up as a merc when she had decided to go down that path instead.

He, of course, had no qualms about accepting his own offer the SAF, the Special Armed Forces, had put forward to him. Worse, Kyli had been completely incensed when he hadn't even had the guts to admit to his own double standards.

*"Just because I think I might make a good SAF doesn't mean that's what I want for my woman,"* he had told her when she had confronted him early in the morning.

*"If it's good enough for you why the hell isn't it good enough for me?"* she had screamed at him, almost in tears. She couldn't understand how he could have done something so underhanded to her. Their private arguments over the directions she wanted to take herself and her career had been one thing, yet purposely tampering with her application had been over the line in her books.

She had walked out after that argument. Walked out of his lodging and straight onto a cruiser to the furthest merc assignment she could find.

Six months later, covered metaphorically if not literally in blood and gore, she had returned. Careful probing of her former wet team mates had netted her some vague knowledge, but not enough to satisfy her.

Much like Gregor before him, Max had been whisked away on a cruiser into the stars for more in-depth training and never been heard from again.

She had visited her family, closed up her musty and memory-laden lodgings, left a few prized possessions with her parents and packed up the rest of her gear. Selling most of her stuff she ended up with a fistful of credits, one large duffel bag of clothes and odds and ends, and had headed back into the ever-expanding sky of the galaxy.

Following the stars, fighting to help set up new colonies and free those under oppression, she discovered that seven years passed supremely quickly, as if in a blur. Now she found herself damn near thirty and while maybe slightly more cynical than the dewy-eyed, fresh-faced wet recruit she had been, she felt a hell of a lot more tired than any self-respecting twenty-nine-and-a-half-year-old ought.

Sipping a tiny amount of her fourth, and most definitely last, Blue Vodka, Kyli let her mind wander.

If she had to, she would return to the mecs, yet a part of her ached to settle down in the one spot. Most mercs didn't last more than a few years on the trail. It took stamina and a mental fortitude to aimlessly wander wherever one was placed.

Kyli admitted freely she had enjoyed the life of a merc, yet over the last year she had been caught twice unawares, resulting in being beamed and worse. The most recent time, on her second-to-last assignment it had taken more than a month of intensive healing before her arm had been patched up.

Modern technology being what it was, not only had all thirty-odd bones of her palm and wrist been mended along with her multiple-times broken arm, but no scarring remained to remind her of the truly awful injury. Even so, nothing could take away the fact her arm and wrist now ached in the cold and her strength was no longer as full as it had been previous to the wound.

Training and sheer determination had done much to restore her body as it should be, yet she could no longer kid herself she was "good as new". Kyli knew enough to realize that one day she would be concentrating on her aching arm and not the fight she fought. Seasoned merc as she prided herself on being, she knew when to quit before she found herself hurt even worse.

Grimacing, determined to not wallow in her own personal brand of self-pity, Kyli raised her shot glass in a silent toast to fate, the goddess, and herself. She had survived and survived well these last few years. She knew her own strengths and weaknesses better than she knew her own name. She knew her body and her limits.

Now all she needed was a delicious fuck-buddy for the next few days and nights as she tried to wheedle her way into the Force. Which particular branch she would aim to ingratiate herself in she still felt hazy on, but a few hard-core rounds of sex to get the lust dragging her down out of her system and her life would be complete and her world could continue on its correct path.

Sitting up straight, with her new course all planned out in her mind, Kyli smiled.

A fuck-buddy.

Now that she had returned home and truly decided to remain here, finding a short-term sexual partner couldn't possibly be too hard —

*Oh goddess, no! Not here, not now* —

Kyli resisted the urge to duck underneath the table where she sat. As if her stroll down memory lane had conjured them, Gregor and Max stalked towards her. Interestingly enough, other members in the bar almost seemed to sense them coming. People moved out of their way, practically opening a path between the two men and her small table. It looked extremely cool. Kyli just watched for a moment. Her pride insisted she stay and not duck or worse, run for cover.

Even though the two men had entered the seedy bar together, they now separated in opposite directions so their large bodies honed in on her table, one coming down either side of the room. Many people glanced at them curiously and then far more speculatively back at her. Kyli wondered if she would be helped or hindered if she lost her mind and tried to escape.

The intense, predatory manner of their stalking showed her more clearly than a shouted warning how serious they were. She instinctively knew flight would be useless.

Not that she wanted to flee, yet something deep inside her knew this wouldn't be a usual reunion. The intensity of their look, the masculinity that came from both of them like shock-waves simultaneously warned and drew women like magnets.

Oddly enough, they seemed to still work perfectly together. They had always been good friends, even back in the wet team. They somehow sensed similarities in each other, and it had bonded them together in a friendship that had never wavered. Or it had never wavered to her knowledge.

With the ease and familiarity these two worked together, she seriously doubted anything had changed between them, friendship-wise.

Max's dark skin and deep, dark brown eyes glinted wickedly in the dim light. Gregor's smoky, silver eyes pierced her, sharper than any short-sword. Kyli swallowed, schooling her face so none of her feminine fear or excitement showed.

Fantasizing and reminiscing about these two was one thing, easily done in the privacy of one's head. Having to verbally spar with either of the men was daunting enough. Sparring with both men together might prove to be explosive.

As they closed in on her, Kyli threw the entire shot down her throat, swallowing it down with barely a flicker of her eyelids.

The fact the dark blue liquor burned a path down her throat and rested in a burning hole inside her stomach meant nothing. The fact she wondered if she had burnt a permanent hole down her esophagus also meant nothing. Proving she hadn't lost her guts from her time as a merc was all that mattered.

"Still challenging everyone around you I see, Kyli," drawled Max, pulling up a chair on her left. Raising an eyebrow she nodded at the man. Turning to her right, Gregor bent down to kiss her cheek in greeting.

"Long time, G," she purred, finding it much easier to slip back into their relationship. She felt startled at the heat and wariness encompassing her about Max. Even though she hadn't seen Gregor in more years than Max, theirs had always been an easier relationship than the explosive sexual and deeply personal relationship she had cherished with Max.

While the sexual intensity was just as great between Gregor and herself, time and maturity had shown her their love for each other was more of a friendly love, less potent somehow than what she had shared with Max. The silver glint of his eyes easily showed his humor in their situation.

"I was deep undercover these last few years, that's why I dropped the contact, sugar."

Kyli felt the smile creep over her face. Much as always Gregor cut through all the crap and hit upon what felt important.

"I didn't doubt you," she insisted, smiling at her old friend.

"When I met up with old Max here, right in the finishing stages of the game, we hooked up. Came back here to join the regular Force and settle down a bit. We happened to see your application, which we placed back for reassessment by the way, and the two of us thought a small reunion might be...*interesting*."

Kyli blinked at the innuendo dripping from his last comment.

*Interesting how?* her brain asked, intrigued for the first time in ages. She couldn't tell if it was effects from the Blue Vodka she had consumed, the potency of the men on either side of her, or maybe a combination of both.

Sitting back, moving her chair back so she could see both men without having to turn her entire body, she took a good look at Max for the first time.

He was just as big as he had always been, well over six feet tall and built of solid muscle. Time and most likely his job had worn a few creases into his brow and near his eyes. Yet just like Gregor, he had aged indecently well.

His uniform clung to his muscled body, making Kyli's mouth, and other parts of her body, water. The black material seemed to somehow enhance his dark good looks. Nor had he lost that presence Kyli had always loved about him. He resonated with the innate knowledge he could do anything, and do it perfectly.

That, mixed with his innate masculinity, would be more than enough reason for half the bar to give them a wide birth.

A scantily clad femserver, whom Kyli felt almost positive doubled as an escort after hours, rubbed herself against Max as she dropped another shot of Blue Vodka in front of her. With a delicate eye wiggle the "server" let Max know in no uncertain terms her availability.

Feeling like the fresh recruit she was far from being, Kyli repressed the instantaneous flare of jealousy. Oblivious to the femserver, Max nodded down at her shot.

"Lucky for me I can afford this now. What number is it?"

"I didn't order another," she started grumpily, only to be cut off by Max.

"I ordered a refill for you of whatever you were having. Are you still a three-er?" Kyli felt heat enter her face. She honestly couldn't even remember the last time she had blushed like a virgin.

It was just...the way he had caressed the word *three-er*.

It had been a huge laughing point among their wet team that Kyli became unreliable after her third shot. Didn't matter if it was mother-milk draught or the most expensive Purple Vodka money could buy—three shots and Kyli became worse than a giggling groupie.

Kyli sat up straighter and, determined to prove her balls if nothing else, looked Max straight in the eye. "I'm not that giggly young thing anymore Max. This is my fifth, and I think I'm doing a damn good showing for myself."

Kyli internally breathed a huge sigh of relief to hear no slurring in her words. She felt by no means drunk, but she still had a tendency to slur her words after her third potent drink.

As Max grinned wickedly at her, obviously trying to get a rise out of her, Kyli caught the meaningful, scorching glance shot between the two men. The glance between them made her pussy moisten even more, yet instead Kyli concentrated harder on his words.

There had been something in the way Max had spoken, the dark and erotic manner of his words that had heated visions of the three of them writhing in pleasure upon his king-sized bed run scandalously through her mind.

Inordinately pleased to see her hand *not* shaking, she picked up the shot glass.

"I'm not the little wet recruit anymore," she repeated strongly, she enunciated the words clearly so they would not slur. "I've seen quite possibly more of the galaxy than either of you."

Smiling smugly at each man's raised brows, she took a small sip of her vodka. No sense in getting smashed just yet. If nothing else she felt incredibly grateful for the knowledge that Max and Gregor had resubmitted her application. With that knowledge the future looked a helluva lot brighter than it had previously. Besides, the men obviously had something they wanted to talk to her about, so she might as well stay and listen to them.

"Obviously I haven't seen the same darker sides you have, thought I *have* seen more than my fair share of the human and other forms of corruption everywhere. Still, I'd bet plenty of credits I've traveled further and seen more than either of you."

Slightly startled, she smiled as Gregor leaned toward her chair, brushing her dark locks from her shoulder.

"I am sure you've seen more places, sugar, yet I doubt you've overcome your three-drink rule."

Kyli frowned. What was this thing the boys had with three? This had been the second time the boys had placed undue emphasis on the word *three*.

Was is just her slightly blurred senses? Or her imagination? She barely resisted when Gregor reached out and removed her shot glass from her hand.

"From the excessive dilation of your pupils, and that very faint slur you're trying so hard to hide, sugar, I'm betting you don't want any more vodka tonight, blue or otherwise."

Her frown deepened. "What right —?"

She didn't even get to finish her complaint. Gregor held the shot glass out to Max, who easily accepted it. Kyli couldn't tell what he did with it, however, as Gregor held her face toward his and kissed her.

Kyli closed her eyes, could hardly believe she still felt the childish wonder of his kiss. The years melted away as if they had never been, and Kyli was once again the young, fresh-faced recruit, eager to save the world and explore the galaxy.

Gregor had always been a kick-ass kisser. Kyli's hands reached up to run through his short hair of their own volition. Feeling the silky smooth strands run along her fingers made her moan.

As always, Gregor took all she had to offer. When her mouth opened on her moan, he slipped his tongue inside her, relishing the easy conquest.

Kyli felt the familiar whirling sensation, of being caught in her own web of dreams and fantasies. The familiar lust and easy response felt like an old robe being slipped back on after a long time without it.

It was as Gregor reluctantly pulled away that she recalled her surroundings. Panting lightly, she turned to survey the room, finally resting her eyes on Max. His face seemed etched with hunger, desire. The raw need she used to see often. She flushed slightly, unused to feeling so gauche and unsure of herself and her actions.

"I-I didn't mean to..." she trailed off. She flatly refused to apologize for something she had enjoyed, and something he had no right to feel annoyed over. Yet neither had she meant to tease or taunt him.

Turning, she looked at Gregor, unsure what the hell was going on. He licked his lips in a happy, satisfied manner.

"You taste of Blue Vodka and passion, sugar. Nice to see some things never change."

She smiled. Taunting banter she could do easily.

"I never used to taste of Blue Vodka. I couldn't afford it back then."

Amusement deepened the laugh lines around his mouth.

"I was talking of the passion, and well you know it."

Shrugging, Kyli turned back to look at Max.

"Some things never change," she said softly.

For the first time, she saw the amusement as well as the hunger deep inside Max's eyes. He looked as if he had been starved, and for a moment she wondered if she was seeing things. As quickly as she had seen it, the hunger and amusement were both banked.

"And some things simply get better with age. Come back to my lodgings, Kyli."

Hesitating, not wanting to make a decision, she looked back to Gregor. He simply smiled and sat there.

"Uh—" she procrastinated. She desperately wanted to catch up with both men, yet she wasn't exactly sure how to explain it without offending either or both of them.

"Gregor and I just want to catch up on old times with you. We flipped outside and I won, so my apartment it is." Max explained. That comment in itself showed her how he had matured.

The old Max rarely if ever explained his actions. The concession spurred her into action. Nodding, she picked up her beamer and stood. A nanosecond of dizziness, and then she felt fine. Somehow both men must have noticed her split second of unsteadiness. Simultaneously, they both gently grasped an elbow each.

"You were really guzzling down those vodkas, weren't you, sugar?" Kyli couldn't help but smile at the laughter in Gregor's voice.

"I was just remembering old times and commiserating over my non-acceptance at the Force. Plotting my Plan B."

"We can plot together back at my place," Max threw in, amusement deepening his voice. "I'm sure something will come up between the three of us."

Kyli noted Gregor could hardly contain his snort of amusement at Max's words.

"Something will definitely come up," he added, almost as if he were speaking another whole different conversation with Max.

Before Kyli could comment he hastened to add, "We have a bundle of experience between us, I'm sure we can think up any number of plans."

Eying each man warily, Kyli waved to the bartender, who nodded to her.

"I've already debited my drinks, as long as you covered that last one," she said as Max nodded.

Feeling as if she were caught in a dream, or maybe a time-warp, she allowed the two drop-dead handsome men to each place a hand each on her shoulder to gently guide her outside the bar. Opening her mouth to initiate some banal chatter, she gasped as they almost immediately halted beside an obviously expensive Cruiser.

It was the latest, top-of-the-range machine in what commonly had been labeled "brick red". The color alone was indecently expensive as the pigments needed to create the color were not only off-world, but incredibly hard to come by, as the flower they came from only bloomed on the evening of every full moon.

Little as she knew about Cruisers, it was patently obvious it was an indecently expensive machine.

"Whose?" she queried shortly, not wanting to make a big deal out of letting them take her back to Max's. Gregor smiled in masculine pride and possession.

"Mine," he said simply. Kyli nodded as Max opened the door and moved the back of the seat for her to fit in. Kyli slowly and carefully strapped herself in as both men followed suit with a casual ease that spoke better than words. They had indeed been spending time together of late.

Mulling happily over what this could signify, she watched the city speed by in a fast blur. Neither of the men talked, so she felt quite happy to let the comfortable silence enfold the Cruiser.

When Gregor pulled up outside a small residential block, Kyli felt a spurt of surprise fill her.

Since when had Max become a homebody? Shelling out a hell of a lot of credits for the land and residence didn't strike her as the Max she remembered.

Looking closer at the decadent residence, Kyli guessed he had probably called in a few favors as well. The land and privacy of all the trees and foliage surrounding the lodgings would not have been easy to come by, and practically impossible for an "average" person.

While greenery wasn't illegal, concealment of properties and personal lodgings were severely frowned upon. One needed highly placed government connections, not to mention Force connections simply for the permits of such things.

If she didn't miss her guess Max had spent considerable amounts of time, effort and exertion of prestige to gain this abode. She reminded herself once again that a number of years had passed since any of them had been in contact. For all she knew he had been contract wedded and split a dozen times, with half a dozen brats around his ankles.

A dark chuckle from Max brought her thoughts back into the Cruiser.

"I bought it for myself earlier this year when I came out of deep cover. I wanted something permanent, something mine," he explained. Kyli smiled in gratitude for the explanation.

"It's lovely," she commented truthfully, refusing to name the warmth creeping through her at the knowledge he wasn't bonded, yet. The size of the lodging more than anything showed her he planned to get bonded sometime in the future, but he certainly wouldn't have said he bought it for himself if some other woman was in the picture.

"You think?" he replied cryptically. Kyli rolled her eyes and caught Gregor's laughing expression in the mirror.

"I thought you were the master of encryption?" she commented idly to him. She felt even more surprised when he answered her. Gregor used to keep the bulk of his responses to physical answers, touching, and caressing.

"Max and I have been learning from each other these last few months. Sharing a few of our skills and knowledge. We've become good friends again."

Kyli frowned.

"You've always been friends, ever since wet training."

Gregor cast a look at Max and they shared a masculine grin. They obviously both were fully aware of the undertones the night held, and knew whatever they meant. Their grins spread into laughter and they both exited the Cruiser. Max again held the door open for her, and she frowned in confusion over this.

She might have drunk a few Blue Vodkas, but it was obvious she no longer became falling-down drunk after a couple of drinks. She was not inebriated. She knew her mind was clear and working madly to solve the puzzle the guys presented. Neither was she slurring her words, or walking unsteadily.

So why the extra special service?

*Is it so hard to believe he's just being a gentleman?* her mind whispered. Kyli decided to enjoy it for the gesture it was. She smiled politely and thanked him. Standing straight, she threw off her own doubts and caution.

"Let's just say we've shared a lot of knowledge and we're determined to reap the benefits of it." Max said deeply, grinning down at her darkly.

Kyli looked from one man to the other and knew that was all the information she would get out of them for now. Her gut churned in excitement and wonder of what the night held. She would find out soon enough whatever scheme the boys had cooked up. As they crossed into the small residence she decided to roll with the punches and maybe even try to surprise the men herself. She could feel the eager excitement inside her build.

Besides, rolling with the punches in the unexpected was what a merc did best.

# Chapter Three

Kyli sat on the edge of the couch, right in one corner, trying not to squirm in her bare feet. As with any residence, everyone had removed their shoes upon entering. Even if she hadn't known the etiquette before entering Max's residence, the plush carpet would have told her quite plainly the expense and time Max had put into his residence would necessitate the removal of one's shoes.

She couldn't help but feel that both Gregor and Max had been stalking her, surrounding her, ever since they had entered the bar. She had no problem with feeling cornered or stalked. In her career she had felt it practically every day. A female merc got used to the feeling and dealt with it.

Yet she wasn't used to feeling surrounded and stalked *sexually*. Or she hadn't since she had last seen these men. With Gregor she felt used to him pushing her limits, the feeling of being taunted and drawn as far as she could deal with. With Max she felt used to being claimed, to belonging to him, to the possessiveness of his masculinity.

Both men were used to touching upon her desires and needs sexually, and that seemed to have only increased over the years they had been apart. Gregor had always had the uncanny ability to tap into her deepest and darkest fantasies. He had been able to scare, interest and tease her to the point of climax with his voice and hands alone. He had also always known exactly what to do or say to make her drenched for him.

It had been one of the reasons they could both separate with so little pain. In small doses having someone who knew the inside of your brain and heart so intimately was wonderful. Over an extended period of time it became an overdose of a good thing.

On the other hand, she now realized Max had always held her heart. He was a good man, dedicated to doing only the best for his and everyone else's worlds. The fact he could make her scream with pleasure in bed and wring her dry sexually just added to the bonus of their chemistry.

Max always managed to make her feel very fragile and very feminine.

*Both men…*

She jerked her head up, looked from Max who rested against the doorframe, to Gregor who sat perched on a chair opposite her.

She desperately tried to think of something to say. "Oh boy!" seemed too juvenile, "Yippee" was way out. "You're kidding me," seemed too cynical and uninterested.

*So are you interested?* her brain teased her.

Kyli looked at each man speculatively and chewed her lower lip in contemplation.

"Took you long enough to work it out, sugar," Gregor drawled. Kyli looked to him, looked at his interested posture and relaxed pose.

"You guys knew what you were referring to. Personally I think I'm doing damn well to just keep up with you. Most other people would have taken a while longer."

"You've never been just 'another' person Kyli, and well you know it," Max said, not even budging an inch from his spot against the door. Kyli knew she would have to make the first move with him. He might have caused the end of their relationship in her mind, but she had been the one to walk away, not he.

She looked him right in the eye, facing him and the situation before her in her usual, straightforward manner.

"You didn't used to share," she stated, letting him take it as he would.

The grin he shot her spiked her system more than the most expensive vodka ever could. It was an engaging, possessive, purely masculine grin of triumph.

"You're not the only one to have grown older and wiser. I might be essentially the same man, but some of my...tastes...have matured over the years."

Kyli felt trapped, ensnared, in Max's dark chocolate-colored eyes. With great difficulty she tore her gaze away and returned to Gregor's cool silver eyes. Questioning him without even needing to say a word, she felt herself relax as he smiled at her.

Obviously the men had arranged something. She couldn't deny the excitement at the thought of having both men possess her. After all, it wasn't every day that a woman's two favorite lovers offered to share her.

Or usually not without a huge blood fight. A girl had to take her fantasies where she could. A hidden whisper of memory touched her mind. Looking back up at Gregor she cocked her head and smiled at her old lover and friend.

"You remembered? After all this time?"

He grinned, showing his teeth. At that instant she could well understand the predator that lurked within him.

"Some things you never forget, sugar."

Smiling, Kyli nodded. She could well believe that. Some things never truly left your mind. She couldn't help the invitation in her eyes as Gregor came to sit next to her on the couch.

"We're really going to do this?" she asked one last time. It had been such a fantasy of hers, as far back as she could remember really, to share her body with two men simultaneously. She had never really pictured this moment, never really concentrated on anyone except her current lover.

Yet the fantasy had always persisted.

She could recall describing her fantasy in loving, explicit detail to Gregor early one morning, after hours of satisfying themselves. She felt amused and touched he had always remembered this particular fantasy.

"Oh yeah," he murmured quietly as he bent in towards her. Angling his head in, he kissed the sensitive spot just under her ear, whispering the words to her, making her hot. Gregor had always had such a skill in this area with her.

"The three of us are going to do this. We're going to do this all night long until you can't even waddle, let alone walk, from the strain in your muscles. We're going to do this until you scream from the pleasure, and then scream from the need for us to stop and let you rest."

Kyli started to pant, felt her eyes glaze over. How easily she could remember doing just that, with both Gregor and Max, separately until tonight, of course. She felt her nipples tighten in excitement, in anticipation of what they had in store for her.

She moistened her lips, wishing he would hurry up and kiss them instead of her neck.

"See?" he teased her, making her want to groan with the need to touch him. "You're already hot, I bet you're already wet too, aren't you?"

Kyli choked down a laugh. Of course she was damp! She had two incredible studs within reach, and both of them were aching to slide inside her. One of her deepest, darkest fantasies were about to become reality, and he asked if she was wet?!

"I'll take that for a yes, then, sugar."

Kyli finally moaned as he took her lips. Just like in the bar, he felt strong, firm. His lips were warm and soft. Unable to hide her rising excitement, and not even knowing why she should, she moved closer to him on the couch and raised her hands to his face.

Cupping him, enjoying the rough texture of his skin and stubble, she lost herself in the myriad of sensations. When he cupped the side of her face with one of his hands she felt delicate, feminine. He let them both drop back slightly, so he lay reclined on the couch and she lay half over him.

She didn't realize until he angled her face, kissing her fiercely and opening her mouth to let his tongue slide inside her warmth, but Gregor had positioned them precisely so that Max could see them from where he stood.

As soon as she thought this she could *feel* the intensity of his eyes, his heated gaze, upon them. Strangely, it turned her on even more than the heat of Gregor's kiss. The knowledge that her lover watched her enjoying another man's kisses fired her blood like nothing she had ever previously felt.

When Gregor palmed one of her breasts beneath the merc shirt she had donned earlier in the morning, she could feel the heat of his hand through the thin material. She arched into him, her breasts aching to be freed and fondled, her nipples tight and scratching against the thin material.

Losing herself in the sensation, feeling her mind fall deeper into the lust Gregor inspired, Kyli couldn't help herself. Noticing her hands finally shook, she removed Gregor's black shirt. Throwing it onto the floor, forgotten before it had even crumpled, Kyli reacquainted herself with his chest.

Gregor had filled out in the intervening years. He had been no raw youth when they had been in wet training. He had been the oldest of the lot of them at twenty-five, yet he had been tall and lean.

Now, as a man on the darker side of thirty, he had a solid bulk of muscles and not an inch of fat on him. Lightly sprinkled chest hair, similar to what she remembered, covered his chest and made the texture of his skin intriguing.

Kyli couldn't help herself, she pulled her mouth away from the teasing playfulness of Gregor's, and ducked down to taste his chest. Small, nut-brown nipples hid amongst the hair. Kyli trailed her tongue along the lines of his pecs, marveling at how different the masculine body was from the woman's.

When she felt a familiar hand behind her, spanning her waist, she couldn't help her gasp. While she had been tasting and reacquainting herself with Gregor's chest, he must have signaled Max. She would know Max's hands, his scent, his heat, anywhere. She nearly choked on her own breath when he moved his hands down to either side of her hips and aligned his crotch with her ass.

He had always loved taking her from behind. She very clearly remembered him aligning them exactly such many times before. It never failed to arouse her, and it certainly worked now.

As Max reclined behind her on the couch he started to nibble on her neck. Gregor pulled her face up closer so he could again start to kiss her and suckle on her lower lip.

"Did you know," Gregor told her, his voice husky with desire, "that whenever you're nervous or thinking deeply you nibble on your lower lip? It's the most distracting thing."

"Just like," Max interjected, "when she's trying to figure something out she sometimes even sucks her lower lip inside her mouth, usually to gnaw on it. It's very distracting indeed, makes a man want to suck it for her."

Kyli laughed, pulled her lips away so she could look down at Gregor. Max still strung kisses down her neck, wrestling with her shirt to remove it.

"It's rather weird to have the two of you talking about me while we're doing this."

"Well," Gregor started, always happy to play the gentleman in the beginning, "what would you rather talk about?"

She heard the muted *rip* as Max tore her shirt from her body, impatient with trying to work out how to remove her shirt without damage.

"Ah," he gloated, tossing her shirt onto the floor with his own and Gregor's, "Kyli doesn't always like talk, she prefers action, isn't that right?"

Kyli felt her face flame in embarrassment. It didn't matter she had been about to respond in that exact manner, having it said for her was humiliating. Before she could even pull away or come to her own defense, Gregor had started laughing in that low, taunting manner of his that made her want to jump him, or hit him. She never really knew which it was.

"I can think of a number of occasions when Kyli enjoyed talking. Or listening to me talk to her. You enjoy hearing a man describe to you what he's going to do, don't you, sugar?"

Kyli felt certain she exceeded mere *embarrassment* when Max laughed as well, agreeing, "I stand corrected. She has always enjoyed listening."

"Are we going to do something other than sit around here making me blush?" she demanded, feeling a bit odd at being talked about like some child who didn't understand the adults around her.

She squeaked when instead of more verbal sparring, as she had expected, Max picked her up from behind, throwing her over one of his shoulders.

Much like Gregor had filled out with depth and muscle over the last few years, so too had Max. He had always been exceedingly tall, with wide shoulders, yet he had filled out in all the right places with impressive hardness.

Watching the ripple of his back muscles as she bounced against him was fascinating.

"What are you doing?" she finally got out, breathless from her upside-down position as much as the erotic masculine scenery before her eyes.

"Doing something other than sit around on the couch," came the terse reply. Kyli lifted her head to see Gregor following them down the hallway. His eyes were alight with eager mischief and desire.

"This ought to be fun," he commented. "And I don't have to just watch," he slapped his palms together, looking like a kid anticipating the Christmas Feast. "I can even join in all the fun and games."

Kyli smiled and shook her head, making herself dizzy.

Before she could even think of a reply, Max entered what was obviously the master bedroom.

Throwing her down onto the king-sized bed, he quickly striped her pants from her and then stepped back. Kyli blinked at the surprisingly speedy removal of her clothes. There had been no extra caressing, no teasing, taunting quality. This more than anything told her how eager Max felt.

Realizing she had become lost in her own musings, Kyli looked up at her two lovers. Blinking, she saw a very naked, exceedingly aroused Gregor perched on one side of the bed. Unashamedly staring, she reached out to touch the tip of his fully erect cock.

Gently running her finger around its tip, she picked up the pearl of pre-cum and spread it over the deep-red head. Licking her lips, she remembered well the deep, stretchingly full feeling of having him thrust inside her over and over again.

At a solid nine inches long, and quite thick, Gregor had been almost the largest of her lovers. When her eyes lifted, his greedy gaze met hers, letting her know he knew exactly what she had been thinking about.

Looking to her other side, she saw Max shed the last of his clothes, letting them fall heedlessly to the floor. As he crawled onto the other end of the bed, she felt surprised at the heat and intensity of her desire.

Sure, she had thoroughly enjoyed both these men in her past, and she now knew she still had unresolved issues with Max. The electricity between them, the sexual tension could be cut with a knife. Yet it was the fact these men were happily about to give her one of her fantasies that had her ensnared in their web.

The three of them were naked, primed and on-the-edge-of-desire ready on a king-sized bed. It was her most secret, darkest fantasy come to life and she couldn't wait to get started.

# Chapter Four

Kyli decided she should be the first to move. This was her fantasy, and even though not at her instigation, she felt it best if she started.

For the first time that night she turned to fully face Max.

"I know how you feel about this sort of thing," she began, not wanting to break the spell, yet neither did she want him to feel pressured. "So if you have any hesitations—" He cut her off, dragging her closer to him so they were practically spooned face-to-face on the big bed.

"We started this," he indicated himself and Gregor, "and I'm a big boy now. I can take the consequences of my own actions."

Kyli smiled as his mouth descended on hers. She shivered as she felt Gregor come up behind her. Drowning in Max's kiss, she only vaguely heard the *snap, click* of a tube of lubricant being opened, and then shut.

An instant later she twitched in surprise as she felt his wet finger probe her anus. She gasped as he slid the slick digit inside her to the first knuckle.

"Oh, man…it's been so long!" she moaned, overcome with the remembered feelings. Gregor had been the first man inside her hidden passage. The first and, to date, only man inside that particular orifice. From his grunt of pleasure and the way he twisted the digit, he realized it too.

"This is so tight, sugar. No man has been here since me, has he?"

Kyli could only moan as he stroked her inner walls.

"Has there been anyone else, Kyli? Answer me."

"No," she moaned against Max's mouth, the tone of Gregor's voice insisting on a response. "No man has been there since you, Gregor."

Gregor grunted with a purely masculine pride and ego.

"He's going to teach me every nuance of how you like having that beautiful ass of yours reamed, Kyli, and then no other man but *me* will ever be in there," Max said with strong possession in his voice.

Kyli felt her heartbeat accelerate at his words. She couldn't tell if he meant it seriously, or just in fun. If the look of depth and possession in his eyes were any indication, he was all business.

"Yeah, baby, I mean it. Tonight is all for you, but afterwards…" he let his words trail off, his meaning pretty clear.

Kyli felt her breath come in pants and her pulse flutter wildly. He meant to claim her. Her feminine pride pricked. He obviously thought she'd be an easy conquest. How very wrong she would prove him.

"Not that it matters where I'm going," Gregor teased as he rubbed his shaft against her ass, screwing his thick digit even further inside her, stroking her thin anal walls, "but you have had your suppression shots, right?"

Kyli nodded. She couldn't help shivering in delight at the electric sensations screwing through her system from his probing. It felt wonderful, but odd to be feeling a man's thick, strong finger stroking and opening, stretching her hidden passage, yet simultaneously being held by Max and seeing his carnal intent clearly in the depth of his eyes.

"Sure," she replied huskily, having a heap of trouble keeping her mind on the conversation and not on Gregor's thrusting finger or the heated possession in Max's eyes. "It's standard regs. All women have to keep up-to-date on their pregnancy suppression shots. I had mine a little while ago."

"Excellent," rumbled Max, satisfaction positively oozing from him. "Then we won't need to worry about any slip-ups."

Kyli raised her eyebrow. "I assume both your health checks are clean?"

"But of course," Max purred, leaning back in to cup her breasts and claim her mouth. The dark, spiraling lust engulfed her. For what felt like hours she knew they had been skirting around their deep, electric feelings of lust. It had always been like this between them.

The tension, the waiting, ready-to-pounce quality always flowed thickly between herself and Max.

When they weren't screaming at each other, or throwing manuals and dishes at each other, they were fiercely clenched in the most intimate of embraces. Pushing each other sexually to do more, to be more with each other.

Kyli finally stopped fighting herself and let the black ocean of lust and desire wash over her, encompass her. She arched into Max, dug her nails into his back and clung to him like a life raft. She couldn't help arching her ass back further into Gregor's dark possession, but her chest, her mouth and arms were glued to Max.

Gregor, fully cognizant of the heavy amount of past between herself and Max, nudged her leg so she half-straddled her lover.

"Open up for me, sugar," he coaxed. "Open wide for me like you used to love to."

Kyli couldn't help her moan anymore than she could help her thrill of passion as Gregor screwed his finger inside her to its second knuckle. Max's growl of jealousy brought her attention back to him.

"Ooh," she cooed like some love-sick teenager, enjoying the rare opportunity to tease and poke fun at him, "feeling a little left out, are we, darling?"

Before he could take control of her and the situation again, she lowered her hand to stroke his shaft. Gently, loving the smooth texture of his skin, Kyli stroked him until he grabbed her shoulders to drag her as close to him as possible.

"You're playing with fire, Kyli," he warned her, letting his gaze burn over her features.

She smiled up to him. "Max, darling, I'm always playing with fire. I wouldn't know what to do with myself if I weren't. Move up," she pushed at his chest, indicating for him to scoot up the big bed, "I want to suck you," she murmured, knowing her blunt words would add to his torment, to his enjoyment.

She groaned and bit her lip as she felt Gregor using the lubricant pooling out her gaping ring to lube up his middle digit.

"Gregor," she moaned, trying to warn him, "it's been a long time…"

He chuckled darkly at her pleading, obviously knowing she felt some nerves.

"I know that, sugar, why do you think I'm using the lube?" He slowly inserted his thick middle finger, to the first knuckle, letting his slimmer index finger press all the way inside her split open passageway.

As Gregor stroked her inner walls with decadent skill, she couldn't help but moan at the sensations he spun through her. It had been so long, she had never let anyone except him touch her ass. She hadn't trusted or desired anyone else enough.

Looking up to Max's burning gaze, eagerly devouring her painful pleasure, she knew all that would change very soon. He must have sensed the direction of her thoughts, for he grinned widely, his white teeth in stark contrast to the darkness of his skin.

"Oh yeah, baby, I'm learning everything. Next time it won't be Gregor in your ass, it will be me and only me forever after that. I'm hard with the wanting and can't wait to begin."

She opened her mouth, certain she would deny it. She and Max had been impressive lovers, in truth she loved him still, but Gregor was the only person who would ever truly understand some of her darker desires.

Max must have been talking to Gregor for ages, for instead of letting her deny him, deny their changing relationship, he took the Dark Alpha role she loved her lovers to take, and thrust his cock into her mouth.

Not even thinking about it, she automatically closed her eyes and sucked him hard, drew him deeper into her mouth and attempted to deep throat him as she knew he loved.

Raising her hands, she stroked his balls, rolling the thin-skinned, heavy sacs around in her fingers. When she felt his hot hands clasp either side of her head, she knew he wasn't thinking about his jealousy or anything else except the heat and suction of her mouth.

Raising her eyes, she watched him as he watched Gregor sliding his middle finger inside her to the hilt, stretching her ass and widening it for his inevitable penetration. He watched her ass stretch wide open, and she could see the black hunger raging inside him, the need to possess her, split her with his immense cock deep into her ass. He wanted to be inside her ass, and everywhere else in her body.

Sitting above her as Max was, even thrusting his cock inside her mouth, she knew he could see down the entire length of her body. His eyes flicked from her mouth, as it sucked his huge shaft, to her pointedly erect nipples, begging for a set of clamps, to her hands and then down to her ass and where her creaming pussy hid from his view.

Shivering, she suckled him harder, gently grazing her teeth under his shaft as she remembered used to drive him wild. As much as she could tell he wanted to possess her, she managed to wish for it more. She wanted him to turn into the Dark Knight of her dreams and fantasies, she wanted him to take the dangerous and dominant role he always had held in her fantasies.

The desire she knew he could see in her eyes, coupled with the actions of her suckling mouth and foraging tongue, caused him to drag his gaze away from her body, to peer down at her upturned face.

"I'm going to do that to you, baby," he told her, quiet strength and sheer determination lending weight to each one of his words. She knew he meant them completely. "I'm going to prepare your ass, prepare you, stretch you and lube you up gently. And then I'm going to plunge balls deep into you. And you know I'm bigger, thicker than Gregor—so maybe it's just as well he's preparing you tonight. Because tomorrow..." he trailed off, knowing she would imagine *just* what pleasures tomorrow would bring.

He thrust himself even deeper into her mouth, making her moan around his shaft at the full sensation. She could feel Gregor stroking inside her darkest, most hidden treasure, causing electric pulses of energy to spiral through her.

Amazingly, she could feel her orgasm build. She had a cock in her mouth and two thick, masculine fingers in her ass, and she felt hotter than she had in her entire life. She could feel it build, feel the wash of the power of her orgasm as it steadily grew, larger than anything she had ever previously felt.

She must have made some sort of noise to indicate her growing need, for she felt Max twist his body. His thick, long fingers reached down, down, until he could touch her clit. His change in position made his cock thrust deeper down her throat, until she nearly choked, but defying all expectations, she found she needed, even *craved* the extra penetration he gave to her.

With all the black emotions and needs roiling inside her, she knew she needed his possession in her mouth as much, if not more than, she desperately needed his finger stroking her clit to help her get even closer to that shining, shimmering climax on the horizon.

She knew all the years of feminine affront, of truly being "one of the boys" and only letting herself be slightly feminine in the sanctity of her own small cabin had let much of her already depleted feminine side simply wash away. By surviving in the purely masculine world of a merc, she had buried the small amounts of her femininity and female desires.

Yet right now, with Gregor at her ass, stretching and preparing her for his thick cock, and with the large, utterly loved prick of Max's thrusting balls deep down her throat, she couldn't help the spreading warmth of being cherished, of feeling completely feminine from washing over her.

Kyli felt more alive, more sexy and desired than she had in all the years of traveling the galaxy. Even her secret "personal care" sessions where she had given herself ripping, screaming orgasms didn't even scratch the surface of the dark pleasure she derived from this evening.

The desires she could feel encompassing her here were dark — dark and forbidden. Two men at once? Who truly could say they had experienced such a thing with no doubts, no recriminations and no jealousy? Particularly two men who were such good friends, her ex-lovers, and now workmates together?

Two men who were special to her and who completely understood her sexual desires and cravings.

Knowing she was one lucky bitch, Kyli couldn't help wallowing in the mass of emotions crashing around her. She cherished each and every second she had given to her by these two men. Deep in her heart she knew this was just the one night, the one special, unforgettable night, yet she still couldn't help hoping it never, ever came to an end.

Even so, now she had opened the Pandora's box of her sexuality and re-found and awakened her long-lost feminine side once again, she didn't think she could leave it behind, or shut the box again. Once some things were released there truly was no turning back. This obviously had become one of those situations.

Kyli smiled secretly, deep inside herself. She wondered if Gregor, or more importantly, Max, knew or understood just what exactly they had released when bringing to life one of her most desired and secret of fantasies.

She thought Gregor might have a slight inkling. He had always been uncannily tuned in to her desires and needs, her and every other lover he ever had. The sensual knack he had for reading his lover's mind held a large part behind his immense reputation and was why he always had women throwing themselves at him.

Women talked, boasted, moaned, sighed and generally made drooling idiots of themselves when recounting experiences with Gregor.

Max, on the other hand, had that wicked glint in his eyes that women also sighed over. Yet unlike Gregor it was his dark and dangerous good looks that had women drooling. His dark skin seemed to drink in all the light in the room, while his pure, white teeth flashed like a beacon in the night.

He also gave his undivided attention to whatever held his mind at the time. Within the depth in his dark brown eyes she could easily tell he drank in every single moan, every thrust of her hips as both he and Gregor gave her indescribable pleasure.

Oh, yeah. He knew *exactly* what he unleashed within her, and he loved every minute of it. The twinkle in his eye, the way he sweated and strained to bring her more pleasure, he seemed to want more and even more from her.

"Come for me, baby. Give me everything," he crooned, as if his words alone could make her come. And maybe they could. He squeezed her clit, already fully engorged with her heat and need, and the pleasurable pressure made her world explode.

The heady rush of emotions and heat ran over her, through her. She screamed around his massive shaft inside her throat and felt her juices run over his hand.

It wasn't until she started coming down from her high that she realized Gregor had lubed a third finger.

"Third one, sugar," he teased. "And after that climax I think you can take it. You know a bit of pain always helped you get hot for the second time."

With that, he thrust the third finger inside her ass with no preliminaries. Three fingers inside her, all lubed, fluted and stroking her thin inner skin. It was painful, but the pleasure his caress brought her, the decadent, dark thought of his possessing her ass put such an erotic edge to the pain she couldn't help but be turned on even more.

She felt stuffed full, felt as if any of them moved an inch she would die from the pain — or maybe the pleasure. The two blended together so perfectly she couldn't even tell where one left off and the other picked up.

"Shit," Max breathed, still stroking her clit, "you're creaming like nothing I've ever seen before! Wish I'd known about your kinky side all those years ago. We'd have had some rockin' times."

Even if she had wanted to, Kyli had no idea how she could respond to that. Shrugging her shoulder instead, she continued sucking on the immense shaft still sliding deeply down her throat.

"Max my boy, time for you to watch and learn from the master," Gregor teased, withdrawing his fingers from her ass and scooting across the large bed to where Kyli vaguely recalled seeing a bedside table.

The loss of his fingers, the gaping emptiness in her ass had her moaning in disappointment.

"Shh," soothed Max, still holding either side of her head, thrusting himself in and out of her mouth. "Soon you'll be so chock full of rampant cock you'll never notice this momentary loss. Besides," he continued, thrusting himself as far as he could, so his stomach rested against her nose, "you should be sucking me off. While I'm not complaining of your ministrations to date, you're the only one here who's come so far."

Kyli felt a spurt of feminine annoyance at his words, and moved her fingers from his sacs to the delicate skin just below them. Gently, she pinched the crease there, knowing the powerful effect it used to have on Max. He always came when she did this.

"Oh yeah, baby, lovely to see you haven't lost your touch," he cheered her on, thrusting in and out with a steady force. Enough to heighten her arousal, yet not enough to tip her over the edge just yet.

She felt the bed dip as Gregor obviously returned. He didn't even bother to test her receptiveness again. With her moaning and creaming, fully allowing Max to drive his cock as far down her throat as possible, it looked fairly self-evident she was as primed as possible.

"Let's see," Gregor said, moving behind her. The heat of his body felt so welcome after the chilly air had cooled her skin. "Oh yeah," he purred, running his index finger around her still-pouting anus. "Juiced up and ready to ride. Just how I remember you."

Kyli gasped as Max withdrew his cock from her mouth. She couldn't help herself, didn't even think, she just grasped his hips and tried to pull him back down onto her. Half-lying on the bed though, she had no leverage and he easily captured both her wrists in one of his much bigger hands.

"Uh-uh, baby, this is our show. I know you love it, but I really don't want to manacle you. I want you to have your hands free so you can explore both of us as we take our pleasure in you. But if you're going to be a nuisance, I *will* manacle you."

Kyli thought about it for half a second. While being bound inevitably turned her on, the thought of missing out on touching the two men who had sexually taught her the most, rankled.

She wanted to touch them and participate, wanted to turn them on just as much as she knew they would for her. While at times she loved being bound and at her lover's mercy, she instinctively knew in this instance she wanted to participate as much as possible.

Letting her arms droop, she surrendered to Max. He grinned, white teeth flashing.

"That's my girl, now sit back and let Gregor teach me."

"My pleasure," the man behind her drawled huskily. In one quick, precise movement he spread her ass cheeks wide, aligned his lubed cock with her tiny opening, and thrust himself inside her.

Kyli couldn't help herself, she arched her back and cried out incoherently, at first in pain. But then, as Gregor held himself still and let her body adjust to the massive penetration, she felt his heat seep into her, felt the throbbing pulse of his cock beat inside her back entrance.

Her body, as always, acclimatized itself to his shaft. Her inner muscles began to suck at his shaft, to beg for more. She moaned, unable to hide her delight in the possession. She opened her eyes to watch Max watching her. She could feel Gregor behind her, aligned over her splayed body, his heat penetrating her every cell. Max's eyes were alight, the dark, dark brown burning brightly in his face.

She could feel his pleasure in watching her, in watching Gregor split her wide and her full enjoyment of it. Without even meaning to, she bucked back with a dark eagerness, desperate for more of Gregor's penetration.

Going back to suckling Max's impressive shaft again, Kyli thrust her burning ass back as far into Gregor's warm body as she could, as much as it hurt, the pleasure and heat overrode everything. She desperately wanted more of Gregor's cock up her ass.

"You love it," Max said softly to her, amazed and enticed. "It hurts you like a son-of-a-bitch, but you love it. I wish to hell I'd known all those years ago." Kyli pulled her mouth away from his cock, until she could just lick and lave at its purpled tip.

"You never asked," she teased him. For he had asked many times about her fantasies, her desires, what she loved in a lover. She had answered him, had told him she sometimes liked to be bound by the word-activated manacles the Force and mercs regularly used. She had told him many of her tamer fantasies and desires. Yet never once had she mentioned her enjoyment of anal penetration, or of being physically dominated by a man. She had never confided to him her secret yearning to be taken by two men simultaneously.

Gregor had guessed much of her deeper desires. He had seen the dark, lurking hunger deep in her soul, for it resonated with his own darker needs. No one else had ever seen that side to her.

Except now for Max.

Her mind knew now he understood and acknowledged an integral part of her desires and wants. She also knew he would never let them, or her, go again. She thrilled to the dark, hungry possession, even as she feared it. The fear added to her desire, to her pleasure.

She moaned as Max's mouth came down over hers in a fierce kiss as Gregor finally moved another few inches deeper inside her. The hard, raw pleasure had her crying out her delight and need for more. While she desperately wanted to kiss Max forever, the sensations coursing through her body wouldn't let her wallow in the mouth and taste of the man she loved.

Pulling away from Max, to gasp, to let the immense feelings wash over her, she moaned at the hard thrusts of Gregor's thick cock.

"Oh yes, Gregor, please move deeper," she mewled, unable to think coherently anymore. The wrenching, painful pleasure in her ass burned. She had completely forgotten how intense, how dark and mind-blowing having her ass reamed felt. With Max nibbling and suckling at her mouth and Gregor thrusting inside her ass she felt as if she were in a dream, a fantasy.

She never wanted it to end. She could happily stay like this for eternity.

When Gregor moaned and pulled out, her hands flew behind her of their own accord.

"No!" She panted, grabbing his ass and pulling him back towards her. "Don't go!"

The dark, utterly masculine chuckle embraced her, surrounded her.

Max snorted and held her hips steady with a careless, masculine certainty. Lifting one of her legs up and over his own hips, he opened her for his penetration.

"One," he started, in the steady, commanding voice she instinctively knew he used on his missions. Kyli barely noticed either his word or the following "Two," rumbling through Gregor's chest. She still had her hands around her back, trying to pull Gregor back into her, her mind numb to anything except the dark pleasure of his possession she craved like a drug.

"Three," the men said in unison, and even as Kyli's mind kicked into gear, recognizing what they were doing, she felt herself under siege. She arched up, her body wanting to move backwards into Gregor's embrace as well as fall bonelessly forward into Max's arms as he penetrated her pussy to the hilt.

And she did feel stuffed full. Max hadn't lied or bragged at all.

Gregor, while certainly larger than the average man, filled her ass to perfection. Yet it was Max, with his enormous cock thickly embedded inside her pussy whom she felt pulsing inside her.

Gasping for breath, she closed her eyes as the men set up a rhythm only they seemed to know. In and out they moved, sometimes simultaneously, sometimes one after the other, sometimes completely randomly.

Kyli could only breathe and feel as she felt herself being pushed further and further toward a screaming, earth-shattering, mind-numbing climax.

It was as Max raised his head and drew her pointedly erect nipples into his mouth that she could feel her body draw up, roar towards its climax.

"I think..." she panted, unable but wanting to articulate her screaming, clawing need. "I think..." she tried again, completely at a loss.

Gregor moved his body slightly to aim further inside her ass.

"Come on, sugar, surely you can do better than that," he teased, moving his hands around her sweating torso to touch her clit between her and Max's straining bodies.

His rough finger grazed over her engorged clit, swollen with blood and need.

"I..." she started, not even remembering what she had been trying to tell the men in the first place.

When Max hitched her hips even higher, so her upper body lay mostly on top of his sweating chest, while her lower body lay squashed between Max's thrusting hips and Gregor's large, heated embrace, she felt the different angle of penetration from both men.

Gregor stroking her clit, Max's cock grazed her G-spot and she completely flew apart.

Screaming, feeling as if her head had just exploded, she felt her body seize up as it clenched around both the cocks driving inside her.

As her body broke through the orgasm, she felt as if it splintered into a million pieces, she had one startling moment of clarity. It felt as if she had been handed the keys to the universe and all its secrets.

In that instant, she could see the three of them, straining on the large bed. Max's dark body lay buried to the root inside her much paler one. One of his arms lay around her shoulders, pulling her towards him. The other rested on her hip, angling her for his penetration.

Gregor lay behind her, his back arched like a bow as he thrust his cock into her ass right to the balls. His eyes were squeezed shut in abject pleasure, his face contorted into the mask of a man on the brink of explosion.

She lay in the middle, between her two lovers. The intense give and take they shared symbolized everything that was perfect in a relationship, and simultaneously everything that was fragile.

Kyli lay between the two men like a filling—who had become completely full. Kyli smiled inside at the poetic turn of her mind. A merc never became poetic.

In that single moment of clarity, she felt as if she could answer any question, so full of knowledge and feminine power her head was light with it.

And in that moment she knew with a certainty Gregor and Max could feel each other's cock brushing against both sides of her thin inner walls. Two large, meaty cocks both possessing the same woman, but in different ways.

With Gregor the possession was that of a man satisfying a female's deepest fantasies and desires. With Max, it was that of a liege lord coming home to conquer his chosen Bondmate. Both possessions were delicious, and while Kyli knew she would never forget the feeling of both men driving hard into her, she knew it was Max's possession she craved, needed.

Gregor was a deeply loved friend, but it was Max whom she wanted to spend her life with. As the moment of perfect clarity faded, she realized one last thing. Neither man had yet come.

Feeling the goddess within herself rise, she knew she would from now on always take control of her own destiny, forge her own path. This night and these men had given her that and much, much more.

She tightened her own internal muscles, determined to make both men come.

With a grunt, and then a hoarse shout, she felt Gregor's cock tighten and then explode deep within her ass.

Determined to bring Max with them both, she blindly groped under Max's sac. She stroked and then pinched delicately at his skin, and Max shouted out an alien war cry, followed them over the edge into his own climax and release.

Panting, sweating and feeling as if she had fought a long-held battle or run a marathon, Kyli slumped back onto the giant bed, squashed between her two favorite lovers, and fell into a deep, sated, utterly exhausted sleep.

# Chapter Five

Kyli woke to absolute darkness. Frowning, for a moment she wondered why she was naked and not in her slip. The next question to roll into her still-groggy mind was why there were two other people in the bed with her.

The bar and her two lovers came flooding back to her, filling her senses with images so highly erotic she had to close her eyes to keep them under control. Her mouth watered and already she could feel her pussy moisten in eager anticipation of what would follow.

Snuggling into the bed, she reached out an arm to touch the man in front of her. Short, smooth hair met her touch and she knew it was Gregor. Max had shoulder length dark hair, coarser than the strands entwined between her fingertips.

A thick, heavily muscled arm crossed over her abdomen from the man behind her. The short, coarse hairs on his arm tickled her sensitive stomach. She knew without asking the arm belonged to Max.

He drew her back onto his chest and erect staff. Her ass twinged, wonderfully sated, but definitely a tad tender. She gasped at the sensation and shifted her weight away from the sore inner muscles.

"Tender, baby?" he queried softly. She nodded. "That's fine, we can work with that," he murmured, slipping his half-hard erection gently inside her pussy. She bit her lip, determined not to moan at the pleasure his penetration gave her.

"I've quit my branch of the SAF," he breathed quietly into her ear, not wanting to wake Gregor. Kyli nodded her understanding, even though multiple questions raised themselves in her mind.

After a seconds pause, she knew she had to ask.

"So what will you do now?" she whispered. She could feel the wide shoulders shrug underneath her.

"Probably stay within the regular Force, remain in the one spot. I had pretty much decided to do that when I bought this lodging."

Kyli nodded, remembering a question that had flitted through her mind after something he had said earlier in the evening. "Did you tamper with my application, again?" She heard him chuckle softly, then felt his hand cross over to stroke her clit.

"No, though I was truly tempted to. I want us to work together. If you recall we're a damn fine team. We don't have to be partners in our work, but being in the same section would certainly be a bonus."

Kyli nodded and decided to think more about that later.

"Why did you set this up? There are more conventional ways to meet back up with an old lover."

Again she felt him shrug.

"Gregor and I hooked back up a while ago. We started talking. When he mentioned you, we talked over all that old news. He told me a few things. We put our heads together, and we came up with the idea of not only seducing you, but also of fulfilling one of your fantasies. Why? Complaints?"

Kyli laughed. "You know better. But…you were always so adamant against sharing, always so…rigid, with so many of your thoughts and opinions. Why the change?"

"People grow up, baby."

Kyli nodded, annoyed with his dense, masculine nonunderstanding of the deeper, delicate question she was asking. Sighing internally, she decided to be more brutally honest, even though it was hard to sound brutal when one whispered.

"Yeah, but are you telling me we're going to stay a threesome?" In honesty she wouldn't mind a few more encounters with both these men, but she loved Max, had decided earlier in the evening to try and make this relationship work.

As much as he claimed otherwise, she knew any lasting relationship of his would have to be based purely on him and his woman. Max was a one-woman man, not a sharing soul.

"Hell no!" he insisted, louder than she knew he had meant. She smiled in the dark, knowing he had just validated what she already knew. He lowered his voice to the softer level he had been using. "Hell no, I won't share you on a permanent basis. But as a once-off, why not? Surely you wouldn't want to use Gregor like that."

Kyli snorted. "Of course I wouldn't, I care for Gregor. I suppose I'm just wondering what your great big plan is. You always have one and I can't help feeling like I've entered halfway through the game."

Max shrugged.

"Gregor and I are friends. He's taught me some shit, and I've taught him some shit. Besides, I feel certain that he's looking for something more permanent now too. He's just always had a hang-up about that threesome fantasy you've had, and he jumped at the chance to join in. He swore to me that the two of you were well and truly over, relationship-wise. We'll stay in touch and continue to work together, of course, but that's all I have plans for. You and I," he said, lowering his voice even more in the warm darkness, "are very much back on, and we'll take this thing as it comes."

Kyli smiled and wiggled her ass slowly, enjoying his penetration in her pussy. "I rather like where we are now," she teased. When sharp teeth nipped at her shoulder, she giggled quietly, not wanting to wake Gregor.

"No more. I'm tired and you're sore, we can play some more in the morning, when I can get some healing cream inside you." Max said softly, regretfully.

"But—" she tried to insist, but she found herself rolled closer in to his side, intimately spooned by her lover and still feeling his erotic possession inside her.

"No buts," he insisted, chaining her to his side in his large embrace. "We can hash over some of your *real* fantasies in the morning. For now, we need to gather our strength."

Sighing in contentment, she assented softly and closed her eyes. She felt a keen disappointment when he pulled his shaft from her, but she knew neither of them would get any sleep if he stayed inside her.

Besides, she would hold him to his promise to get some healing cream inside her the following morning. That could prove interesting, considering the eagerness and sensitivity of the place where she needed the cream.

# Chapter Six

When Max opened his eyes again, he could feel dawn had broken. The soft, warm bundle of Kyli in his arms tempted him beyond bearing. Shifting his head, he confirmed what he had instinctively known as soon as he had woken up.

Gregor had woken sometime earlier and left the bed.

Max knew himself well enough to know he wouldn't be able to get back to sleep again anytime soon. Despite the temptation, he didn't want to wake up Kyli. His woman would need her sleep.

With no real other option left to him, Max reluctantly pulled himself away from the warmth of his lover's body. Gently, he stroked a hand down from her shoulder, following the curve of her back.

Clenching his teeth, firming his resolve, he sat up, heaving himself from the bed and away from the temptation of Kyli's pliant, warm body. The numerous things he wanted to do to her, starting with binding her strong but slender hands and lubing up that delicious ass of hers, flitted through his mind.

Even though he had always been a considerate lover, his lust-riddled brain didn't seem to want to comply when it came to Kyli. His brain seemed firmly settled on the fantasy of lubing his randy cock for a second bout of anal sex, yet he knew she needed a bit of time and some healing cream.

For a few delicious moments, he stood over the bed breathing heavily. Images of him claiming and penetrating Kyli's tiny orifice danced temptingly through his head. Finally, he pulled his thoughts away from that fantasy and drew on another one. Of coating his finger with healing cream and inserting his large, thick finger into her tiny, pouting anus.

Max nodded, knowing he needed to be careful of his woman, take her along slowly, step-by-step. He needed to give her time to come to know him again, to grow to love him as he wanted her to. Much as he'd love to be the raping barbarian of her fantasies, he in no way wanted to misuse her. He would need to be patient.

For the last time, his mind begged him to take his own pleasure, to thrust inside her tight ass. For all of five seconds he seriously wavered in his honorable intent. But Max was a man used to hard choices and sticking by them.

Finally, it was the thought of Gregor still possibly being in his house that decided him. He wanted to talk to his friend, and so he held firm in his resolve to let Kyli sleep, and left the bed.

He padded across the floor past where a crumpled shirt lay, and then he moved to his dresser to pull out a pair of trunks and pull them on over his naked, highly aroused body. Digging deeper, he pulled out an old well-worn shirt and donned it, too. Deep inside himself, he knew Kyli would likely need her rest and strength for the coming days. They had always clashed wills, and setting out the boundaries of their new relationship, he felt certain, would take a toll on them both.

Padding out into the hallway, heading towards the kitchen, he could smell the unmistakable aroma of his coffee machine. Obviously Gregor had begun the brew.

Max felt a moment of relief. He wouldn't have to follow his friend back to his place to have a chat.

While talking was not a common masculine pastime, Max valued Gregor's friendship. Even though they had hashed out the previous night numerous times, Max needed to hear from his friend's own mouth confirmation that his feelings hadn't miraculously changed overnight.

Besides, there were other things they needed to get straight as well.

Just before he entered the kitchen, Max felt an overwhelming relief he had stayed strong in his non-seduction of Kyli back in the bed. He had no regrets, had indeed instigated the previous night's threesome with Gregor. Yet being brutally honest with himself, he no longer would want to share his woman. She had received her fantasy, and once was enough for him. He liked Gregor, more than any other man of his acquaintance. But he didn't think himself a big enough man to share his woman again.

Entering through the doorway, he halted for a minute, taking in the scene before his eyes.

Gregor sat at his table, as he had many a night before, and far more rarely in the morning, disheveled and sipping a cup full of the steaming brew. The sun shone in through the opened windows, showing a clear, bright new day had begun.

And it had.

"You don't even need to start, Max," Gregor drawled, taking another sip of his coffee and pushing aside the morning edition of the holo-news. "After working together for so long, and socializing even longer, I have you pretty much worked out. I know you won't share her anymore.

Frankly it doesn't bother me in the slightest. Like I've mentioned only a zillion times before, Kyli and I are well and truly over — we're friends."

Max nodded in masculine acknowledgement and moved to pour himself his own cup of coffee.

He could tell by the way Kyli had reacted to him, to his passion and possession, that while she was fond of Gregor, he didn't hold her heart. He fully intended to keep her heart all to himself forever. He felt relief he wouldn't need to explain this to his long-term friend.

"I know, man, it just could have been an awkward situation," he started, wanting to thank his friend for allaying his fears.

Gregor merely shrugged, a suitable explanation for him.

"So, now you've tamed your love life, we going to talk more about this investigations firm? Or are you canning the idea?"

Max smiled broadly, glad his friend wanted to ditch the previous conversation as much as he did. Besides, it tickled his sense of humor to realize that not only did Gregor want to change the subject as much as he, but he felt just as eager to go over their newest plan.

To almost anyone else, Gregor's tone of voice would have sounded uninterested in the topic of their investigations firm. The very fact he had brought the subject up showed how deep his interest in their new idea ran.

At some stage during the last year of their friendship, both men had become frustrated with some of the regulations the Force held to. Many times both men had come across dealings where they wished, either together or separately, to investigate more deeply.

For numerous different reasons, the Force had always previously been able to squash their interest. One night a month or so ago, while talking about their shared grievances and frustrations over a half-empty bottle of Red Whiskey, they had hatched the idea of opening their own firm.

With their combined connections, both within and without the Force, they could cover almost everything that could possibly crop up between them. Opening their own firm would give them the legitimate claim of being able to stick their noses in other people's business like a couple of old biddies.

The more they had talked about the idea, the more they had liked it.

Opening their own sideline, relating to discreet questioning and investigations, appealed to them both for many reasons. They would only take on the smallest number of tasks, their primary goal to satisfy their own sense of justice and curiosity.

Neither man needed another job, nor a new business, but they were both frankly tired of the "Order from On High" to just let something drop. This new idea solved both problems handily while simultaneously keep them both on their toes. Besides, once a man—or woman for that matter—held too many "did not follow specific orders" notes on their dossier, the cream of the investigations started heading elsewhere.

Neither Max nor Gregor wanted to get too close to *that* line.

Max smiled. Then again, now he had Kyli she would be more than enough to keep his quota of excitement up. He couldn't help but feel it well inside him at the thought of digging deeper into some of his and Gregor's more recent cases.

"I think it's a go. We both know where we stand on the workload, and we can make much of each others skills, you with your computers and code, me with the more black ops side of things. I think it's a great idea."

Gregor merely nodded and took another sip of his coffee. For the first time Max noticed his silver grey eyes were more reserved than he was used to.

"Anything up, bud?"

Max waited patiently while Gregor took another sip of the brew. Slowly, he crossed over to the table and took a seat, indicating his interest. He wouldn't leave his friend until his curiosity felt sated. Besides, he owed Gregor a favor for the previous night.

Gregor shrugged and looked into his murky coffee.

"Just feeling a bit odd, I suppose. It's not that often I hook up with an old lover. Particularly not an old lover whom I'm still on friendly terms with. Feels...odd. Good, but odd nevertheless. Must be getting old."

Max frowned. He didn't really know what to say. He felt an itchy sensation at the thought of maybe having to talk through either his or Gregor's feelings.

"Uhh..." he started, not sure what to say and trying to quash the feeling of wanting to scratch at his arms. Checking the unmarked skin, he resisted the impulse to get up from his chair and pace the room.

Max closed his mouth and cast about in his mind for something reassuring to say. Gregor stared out the window, obviously lost in his own musings. Max felt a trickle of relief wash through him. Maybe he wouldn't have to say anything at all.

Thankfully for his peace of mind, Kyli entered the kitchen, looking gorgeously rumpled. Max felt his worry drain away. At the very least he could now change the subject.

Feeling a pang of sympathy for Gregor, he was about to offer to leave the room and let Kyli talk over whatever the hell bothered him, until he noticed the lightening of his features.

*Damn, the man is way too happy to see my woman.* Even though he still felt worry for his buddy, nothing could induce him to leave the room now. Besides, from the glint of annoyance in Kyli's eye as she headed over to the table, she had obviously overheard some of the conversation, though which exact piece had annoyed her he couldn't yet tell.

Kyli crossed the room to reach the table where they sat and Max could already feel himself harden in appreciation of her spirit and beauty. She was one fine woman, and he knew she belonged to him and him alone.

He would love to get rid of his buddy, chuck him from the house, strip his shirt from Kyli's body and lay her on the table. Logic dictated that if he did that, Gregor would tease him mercilessly for months, if not years, to come.

Shocking him from his fantasies and morning boner, Max felt a completely alien and totally unwanted flash of jealousy sear through him as Kyli bent down to kiss Gregor's cheek.

Before he think or act to do anything, Kyli stood back up and crossed over to sit on his lap. Max managed to get his wayward emotions under control, until she wriggled her ass teasingly in the safety of his lap. What had been a simple morning hard-on threatened to become a rather public display of dominance.

When Kyli looked over her shoulder to throw him a cheery smile, and cheekily wink at him, he knew he had been played like a finely tuned instrument. The flash of unwanted jealousy thankfully passed, and he felt himself revert to normal.

Or as normal as a man could be considering the raging boner pressed closely to silky female skin. With the woman of his dreams wiggling enticingly on his lap he knew his hard-on wouldn't be subsiding any time soon.

Not wanting to start an explanation, either to Gregor who hadn't missed the flashes across his face, nor his love, he became even more grateful as Kyli began to talk.

"Don't worry about it, Gregor. We all know where we stand. You and Max fulfilled one of my most treasured fantasies and I'm forever grateful. We can leave it there."

Gregor nodded and sipped his coffee again, tension in his shoulders Max hadn't even noticed melting away.

"Besides," Kyli continued, "I want to hear all about this investigations thing. Sounds like immense fun. I can help too, of course."

Max smiled into her back, rubbing his face across the giant cotton shirt of his she had pulled on, obviously fresh from his drawer.

"Now baby, we can talk about this —" he tried not to snicker when she didn't even let him finish.

"What's to talk about? I've got heaps of experience to back me up. From the sound of things you guys won't be doing anything too often. I want in."

Gregor and Max exchanged a masculine glance. Max could read the ambivalence in Gregor's face. The very slight shrug of his shoulders conveyed better than words he wouldn't mind either way. Max felt a trickle the respect one feels of true friendship rush through him.

Gregor was acknowledging Kyli was his woman and this was a decision he, or they as a couple, could work out. He wouldn't mind either way and would support their call on the matter.

Max scrunched his face in thought. Mentally, he weighed the thought of having Kyli stick her nose into their business every moment of the day and snooping through his stuff versus just trusting her to keep herself out of harm's way.

It wasn't even really a hard decision when put that way. The cases they looked into mightn't be what he wanted for her, but he trusted her senses and courage. She *had* been a merc for many years and knew how to keep her nose clean.

Besides, deep inside himself he knew it would be far simpler just to let her in on whatever they worked on. She would be satisfied and he had a much better chance of being able to keep her safe this way.

"I want your word that you'll take my advice. Anything I say is too dangerous for you, you steer clear of. Deal?"

Kyli turned on his lap to face him. He stared at her, willing her to understand his feelings on the matter. She made a face at him.

"I suppose so. But remember I'm a big girl, and haven't exactly been locked in a convent safely away somewhere for all these years. I want to be kept in the loop. Otherwise I might just try to look into things myself. Trust and respect is a two-way street. Right?"

Max nodded. "I understand, baby," and he did. He just hoped he could keep one step ahead of her the whole time. Smiling at himself, he felt his confidence return. At least he'd never be bored!

"Should we start with the Remington case? Or do you lovebirds what me to handle it?" Gregor interrupted as he stood to rinse his mug. Max felt grateful his friend didn't stare at them, gave them their privacy.

He dropped a light kiss on Kyli's nose and gestured for her to sit on the vacated chair. No way would he be able to think clearly with Kyli on his lap.

"Yeah, buddy. That one still sticks in my craw. I'm so certain he's involved somehow, drove me mad not being able to prove it."

"Remington?" Kyli interrupted, "I presume we're talking about Im'an Remington?"

Max felt pride, then a brief flare of worry pass through him. *Damn, he was becoming worse than a wet nurse!*

"Yeah," he said slowly, wondering how long it would take for him to get used to not only having Kyli a permanent part of his life, but also the emotions that seemed to come hand in hand with trying to keep her safe. "How the hell do you know of him?"

"Oh," she shrugged carelessly as she rose to start making the morning meal, "he was everywhere I turned on my last mission. I was supposed to help the rebels on Randor—" she stopped at the choked noises Gregor made.

He had taken another mouthful of the coffee, and turned back to the sink to spit it out.

"Bad coffee, G?" she teased.

Gregor looked at her as if she were some new breed of alien species he had just discovered off-world.

"*You* were on Randor helping the Rebels overtake the Ancient government?"

Kyli dropped the *pomas* fruit she had been arranging onto a platter, a spark that served well as a warning to Max glinting in her eye. From the careful schooling of his features, Max knew Gregor had caught it as well.

"Sure I was. Until a day ago I was a merc, remember? A big, mean, nasty fighting machine. Fighting wherever my services were sold. Traveling around the galaxy fighting other people's fights and teaching those who didn't know how to fight. Remember all that?"

Max cleared his throat and wondered for a split second if he dared ask if her monthly cycle would soon begin. The sexual, loving woman they had bedded last night seemed to be disintegrating before his eyes.

"Gregor wasn't reflecting on your skills, baby, I think you both just shocked us. We've both been investigating Im'an for a number of weeks, yet whenever we could verify an arms deal went down, he had an iron-clad alibi. Either attendance at a political party with hundreds of witnesses, or we've personally watched him eating dinner at well-known restaurants with two or three intimates."

Kyli brought the platter of fruit and a third chair over to the table, indicating for Gregor to sit and eat with them. Max watched her pick up a piece of the green fruit, peel it, and look at it from all angles as she wrinkled her brow in thought.

Gregor and Max watched her warily, as if she were one of the old-style magicians about to pull something spectacular from her hat. When she took a bite of her fruit, they both reached forward to take their own pieces.

She chewed carefully, slowly, and they both peeled and began to eat their own *pomas*. Mentally, Max reviewed all the data he, Gregor, and the few other members of their respective Force team had managed to collect.

"Doesn't it seem odd to you that one man could have iron-clad alibis for *all* the times something major occurred?" she finally said, licking the *pomas* juice from the corner of her mouth.

Max felt his own mouth go dry with the desire to lick the juice for her. With a force of will he had never yet needed to employ, he brought his attention back to the task at hand. He could strip her bare as soon as he and Gregor had made their plan of attack. For now he needed to concentrate with his *other* head.

"Yeah, it actually became our first tip-off he really was involved. No innocent can vouch for all the time they spend."

Kyli's brow seemed to clear, and she shrugged.

"Ah well, I know the background of what you're looking into, but I'm not sure you can help. I do, however, have a ton of contacts within the Rebellion. I left simply because it was all but over. By now it probably is over and the old government has been overthrown. Thankfully, the Rebels will treat the masses much kinder than the old regime."

Feeling equal parts relief and disappointment, Max grabbed another piece of the fruit and turned to Gregor.

"So where should we start? We've already looked closely into all Iman's cronies and known contacts. Damn, I wish the dossier had been more in-depth. Those lazy bastards in Data Acquisition must have been about to go on leave when they made his dossier. Holes the size of a meteor in it."

Gregor shrugged, and after Kyli had taken a piece, snagged the last of the *pomas*.

"Maybe that's our first step then, bro. We do a proper, in-depth analysis of who and what Im'an Remington is."

Max nodded, turning the idea over in his head.

"With the right amount of information something should break, or at least give us a solid lead. Can you do that today? We can meet up back at The Corner and go over—" Max halted as Kyli interrupted him.

"He has a half-brother."

Both men stopped, mouths gaping and turned as one towards her.

"Huh?" Max finally articulated.

Kyli swallowed the last of her fruit, licked her lips like the cat that had the cream, and tucked one foot underneath her on the seat. Resting forward on her arms, she stated very slowly as if to a stupid little child.

"Im'an-Remington-has-a-half-brother."

Confusion and annoyance at the Data Acquisition group who had compiled the dossier he and Gregor had been using warred within him. Shaking his head, he threw off the anger, knowing it would do nothing to aid him.

"Maybe if you start at the beginning," he taunted her, his voice low and faintly menacing.

Or he thought it was his menacing don't-fuck-with-me-now voice. Kyli just smiled charmingly, as if he had been down on bended knee begging.

"I told you, I've spent the last six months on that hole of a crater. The Rebels frankly have my full support and sympathy. The old regime was filled with tight-assed, overbearing bullies. They worked the poor underclass to the bone on less than slave wages so that the government and rich could just eat more and become even more fat on their 'earnings'. It was a pleasure to teach the Rebels to fight and overthrow the regime."

Both he and Gregor nodded, well used to the scenario she painted. Similar ones were scattered throughout the galaxy, as they were both aware. Kyli plowed ahead with her story.

"About a month ago, a few of the Rebel leaders and I were out scouting. 'Know thy enemy' is one of the oldest tricks in the book. We were surveying what remained of the regime, and one of the men we could identify appeared to be Im'an Remington." Here Kyli paused for dramatic effect. Max resisted the impulse to strangle, or better yet, spank, the story from her.

Grinning like the imp she was, she lowered her voice as if she were telling ghost stories to a bunch of children.

"Until we realized the man was actually Am'ah Remington, Im'an's half-brother. We cracked into a few files," she shot a guilty look at Gregor, who merely shrugged in unconcern, "and discovered the men looked enough alike to be taken as the one man from a distance. Or, if someone didn't know them well, they could easily pass for twins."

Shrugging, Kyli sat back and looked at him.

"They aren't identical, but they *do* look enough alike that if you were only surveying them from a distance, and not expecting there to be two of them, they could quite easily fool most people. And that's only assuming they weren't *purposely* trying to fool people. Given the circumstances, if they even thought for a moment you or the Force would be watching them, they could quite easily *try* to look like the one man. And then everyone would be in trouble, for it *would* be hard to tell them apart. "

Gregor and Max exchanged glances.

"Well, that explains a lot," Max started, but Gregor had a huge grin on his face and interrupted him.

"And this gives us the perfect reason to re-open the case and kick Data Acquisition in the ass."

Both men smiled. The techs in Data Acquisition had a bit of a "precious" mind-set, easily upset and made to feel indignant. Generally, Management wouldn't upbraid them unless the mistake was large, or unless there were huge consequences to their glitch. This counted as more than a mere glitch.

While the animosity never felt personal, neither could either man even entertain the thought of not getting the precious techs into hot water. Very few Force members would pass up the opportunity to get a little revenge on the delicate techs of DA.

Gregor stood and put his now slightly crumpled jacket on. "I'll head on out, do my own quick search and start the wheels in motion. You have today off, right, mate?"

Max smiled in pure satisfaction.

"Yep. I'll comm you later."

Gregor shook his head, more to hide his large, wicked grin from Kyli than anything else. Max knew his buddy could feel the satisfaction and anticipation rolling from him in waves. Men understood these sorts of things.

Kyli stood up and threw her arms around the large man. As she hugged him tightly, Max felt relieved he only experienced a small pang of jealousy, not the searing heat it had been earlier.

"Thank you. Stay in touch this time?" she half whispered into Gregor's ear. Max smiled, knowing she wanted privacy more than secrecy. He looked idly down to a page of the holo-news and pretended he hadn't heard.

Gregor merely nodded and said in his normal voice, "Yeah, much like Max here I'm thinking of settling down. I just don't think I'm *quite* as ready as Max."

Max stood from the table, relieved Gregor had included him into the conversation. He stepped over to shake his friend's hand. They looked each other in the eye, a masculine understanding passing between them. Max owed him and he knew it.

"I'll comm you," he repeated, knowing nothing more needed to be said.

The three of them walked to the door. Kyli waved to Gregor as he climbed into his Cruiser.

With the door shut behind them, Max let his gaze burn over Kyli.

Alone at last.

# Chapter Seven

Kyli couldn't help the smile that spread across her face as Max closed the door behind him. He looked so possessive, almost as desperate for her as she felt for him.

"You look like I'm the last shot of Red Whiskey in the galaxy," she laughed, "and you've been given ten minutes to live."

Max took a step forward, his dark, handsome face set.

"I feel like it. I could hardly wait to get rid of poor Gregor—to get my hands on every inch of you. I promised you a bit of healing cream, and we both know I keep my promises."

Kyli laughed again and took a step backwards. She wanted a bit of a chase, didn't want to make it *too* easy for him. So she decided to push him and tease him.

"But Max," she sighed dramatically, knowing her over-acting would turn him on as much as it did her, "I'm so tired. I was up really late last night."

Max snorted and took another step closer to her.

"I was *up* far later than you into the night, darling. Besides, if your divine ass isn't sore, then maybe you won't need any help taking me into it."

Kyli laughed again, though with less cheer. Seeing the set determination on Max's face, she swallowed the last of her laughter. She knew deep in her soul he would never hurt her, but she also knew if she pushed him he would certainly push back.

"Umm...maybe I *should* go and get the healing cream."

When Max dived to grab her arm, she squealed in delight, turned and fled into his bedroom. Max slowly stalked her, knowing she couldn't escape him from there. As he closed the door behind him, he surveyed the large bedroom.

A moment later, Kyli exited the bathing chamber holding a small tube of the all-purpose healing cream most people used. She crossed the room to hand the tube to him. She wrinkled her nose in distaste.

"Really, Max, I don't see what's so sexy about placing a bit of cream into my ass. It seemed really sexy when you mentioned it last night. But now..."

"Don't worry, baby. Just strip off and come over to me," he soothed, wanting to set the mood again. Just because *he* felt hard as a piece of iron ore, didn't mean Kyli instantly fell into the mood.

Besides, a large part of him reveled in making her hot, making her squirm and cream for him. He wanted to do that to her, for her.

Max watched Kyli run a hand through her dark curls. He carefully sat on the edge of his bed. He felt glad he had donned his most comfortable pair of trunks and an old, well-worn shirt. He, at least, was as comfortable as he could be under the circumstances of a hard-on that felt as if it might burst any second.

He sat carefully, not twitching or showing his impatience in any way. He wanted to relax Kyli, to soothe her and turn her on. She didn't seem skittish, merely uncertain in the clear light of day.

And then he saw the fire ignite in her eyes. He kept his features even, not letting her realize he had seen the glint of firm intent in her eyes. He could at least *act* surprised with whatever brainwave she had.

In the space of a heartbeat her posture changed. From being vaguely embarrassed, to being a seductive, sexy siren. The change had started in her eyes, they turned more blue, darker and her pupils had begun to slightly dilate.

Then he watched as her posture relaxed, became more sensuous, more carefree. Her arms were no longer rigid, but lax, lazy. Her hips loosened and began to swing, her legs looked like they would melt and no longer hold her upright. Her hands fluttered around the buttons of his shirt teasingly.

And then he knew what she would do.

*Oh, goddess, no! Anything but that!*

Yet as she swayed her body to a tune only she could hear, as she oh-so-very-slowly moved her hand to toy with the top button of her shirt, he knew she would torture him.

He felt his cock lengthen and grow even harder behind his pants. He watched as she swung her ass, as her hair partially covered her face, leaving her half in shadow, half in the light. After what felt like an eternity, she popped free the first button on his ancient cotton shirt, he knew he stood in the way of trouble.

Kyli had closed her eyes as if in ecstasy, and when she rolled her head back, ran her hand slowly, luxuriously over her bared throat he felt his cock twitch in desire to thrust into her, to own her completely. He swallowed and tried desperately to think of anything except popping every one of the damned buttons off the shirt, tearing the bloody thing from her body.

Instead, he fisted his hands in the smooth sheets where he sat.

"Max?" Kyli asked softly, huskily, "Are you going to kiss me where it hurts?" she purred, causing his shaft to positively *ache* with desire.

"Not at first, baby," he replied, clearing his throat. "First, I'm going to slide my finger, with some of this cream, deep inside you."

"Ooh," she moaned, letting her long, soft curls fall over her back. Carefully, definitely knowing how she taunted him, she lowered one hand to undo another button on the shirt. "But that might hurt me, Max," she teased softly. "You wouldn't want to *hurt* me, would you?"

Max felt his patience start to fray. His always iron-clad hold on his control began to slip. He dropped the tube of healing cream beside him on the bed. Fisting both of his hands even tighter into the sheets, he swore one small woman would not tear his patience and hard-won control.

*Not even the woman he loved.* Strangely, the more he thought about it, the easier it became to accept.

"Tempted as I might be, Kyli," he said through semi-gritted teeth, "Any pain I inflict on you, you'll love. I'd never *hurt* you, no. And you well know it."

Kyli opened her eyes to look at him. Still swaying her hips, she let both hands fall to where her cleavage taunted him through the thin shirt.

She popped another button. She knew full well how she teased him, frayed at his patience and strength. And still he refused to lose his control.

"I thought so. But you're so *big*, Max. So *strong*," her grin widened and he knew she wouldn't stop teasing him anytime soon. Not that *that* recognition helped his libido.

"Baby—" Max cut off his words. No way would he tell her to hurry up. His mind knew she simply teased him, taunted him, wanted him to lose his control.

Little did she know *just* how close to the edge he walked. Better to let her work it out herself. For now, he wanted to see how far she would try to push him.

"Mmm…" she throatily murmured, "I like doing this, Max. Did you know I've never stripped like this for any man? I've always been rushed." She pouted charmingly, making him crazy to bite that full lower lip, to suck it into his mouth and do crazy things with it.

Like let it run down his neck and over his body.

"But I think I'm a girl who likes to take her time. Drag out the sensuality of the moment," she continued, letting her hands cup her rounded breasts through the thin shirt.

He merely grunted his assent, hands and cock twitching to claim her, to grab at her and simply plunge into her. His eyes were glued to the slender, pale hands as they caressed her own breasts and then reluctantly move down to the next button.

With the fourth button she undid, the shirt gaped down to the underside of her exquisite breasts. With the healthy showing of her chest, Max felt his impatience heighten as well as the prickling of heat over his skin and cock.

Max felt his hands rise of their own volition, desperately needing to touch her, to bring her closer to him. Kyli's grin doubled in its power and he scowled.

Clenching his fists again, he returned them to their place on either side of him on the bed.

"Kyli," he warned, "I'm about as close to the edge as you want me, strip off my shirt and come here now."

He felt his temperature spike as she pouted again and undid yet another button. Squinting a moment, he wondered how many more there were to go.

"But Max," she purred, her smile huge across her face. Clearly *someone* enjoyed his discomfort. "I thought you had this legendary control. You're the big, bad-assed Special Forces Man. You can do anything and not break your cool."

The manner in which she teased him finally snapped what was left of his control. In a single, fluid motion he stood up and took the two steps he needed to come directly in front of her. He reached out his hands, so they cupped a breast each.

"Hellfire, Kyli. Your breasts are simply perfect." Flexing his fingers, he kneaded the lush peaks, enjoying the sensation of warm, feminine mounds underneath his palms. He could swear he felt the pointed, erect nipples rasp his palms through the thin cotton.

Unable to bear it a moment longer, he grabbed the offending cotton and ripped it in half. He brought each torn segment of the shirt over her shoulders, popping the remaining buttons. He thought he heard a slight snicker from Kyli, but all he could really hear was the blood pounding in his own ears.

Barely pausing to catch his breath, Max swung the now-naked Kyli up into his arms and carried her back to the bed.

"Why the hell aren't you wearing panties?" he complained. He tossed her casually down onto the bed and quickly followed her. The way she lay pliant there turned him on even more, proved to him that she trusted him completely.

He turned her gently over onto her stomach with his big hands, relishing his enormous bed. Snatching up the healing cream he clicked open the cap. Pressing one warm hand into the small of her back, he exerted a small amount of pressure to get his point across.

"Hold still a moment, Kyli. Let's get this cream into you."

He enjoyed both the visual of Kyli's wriggling ass, as well as her verbal complaint.

"These sheets itch my nipples, Max. Why didn't I notice that last night?"

"Probably," he laughed as he squirted some cream onto his index finger, "because you had much more important issues on your mind last night, my dear."

Smearing more cream onto his thick middle finger, he recapped the tube and let it drop down on the floor. Straddling one leg over Kyli's slim hips, he held her still with one hand on the small of her back, and gently nudges her knees to open them a bit wider.

"Get up on all fours, darling," he said, helping to lift her. "Oh yeah," he stared at her ass. "So beautifully rounded, enticing," he continued, almost to himself, "and just the perfect size for a man to grab a hold of."

Bending down, he oh-so-gently grazed his teeth over the fleshy cheeks. He pulled back and smiled at the little squeak that escaped Kyli's mouth.

"Max!" she gasped, shocked.

Unable to help himself, fully back in control of his urges as well as Kyli's body, he ducked back down to take a small nibble of the ass that tempted him so much.

"This is my ass, now, Kyli," he insisted, pulling back. No teeth marks marred her skin, but he would bet a large amount of credits she could still feel the small pricks of his teeth against her skin.

"No one is allowed here anymore except me."

Before she could complain, flare up her righteous feminine indignation, he rested the tip of his index finger against her ass. Slick with the healing cream, it slid in fairly easily.

The tight muscles contracted and clamped down on his greased finger. Her passage felt so tight and puckered he could feel his shaft swell. He coveted her secret passage like nothing else in the galaxy. He wanted to be inside her, to ram his cock into her until neither of them could think of anything else but the intensity of their pleasure.

As his finger stroked, in and out, Kyli moaned his name, her own pleasure easy to see. Max loved the sound of her moaning his name, painful pleasure dripping from her lips and her hips twitching back to let him deeper inside her ass.

He took his time stroking her inner walls, ignoring the enticing way she wriggled her hips, arched her back and pleaded for him to touch her clit, to help her come.

Instead, he circled his middle finger around the still-puckered anal opening. It clamped so tightly against his finger it was as if it had swallowed him whole.

"Going to enjoy my second finger, my love?" he teased, his voice low and husky with his desire and need for her. He slowly, gently, inserted his much thicker middle finger.

For now, he knew, that would be all she could take. Her cries were partly painful, though the heat and need still resided in her tone. Max knew Gregor had reamed her well last night and, much as he coveted her ass and needed to be inside her, he truly didn't want to hurt her. Until the cream had time to heal her delicate internal tissue, he would have to make do with a finger fucking.

And so he decided to give her the best anal finger fucking she had ever received.

When both of his thick fingers were in as far as they could reach, he began to stroke her inner walls. The long, smooth strokes were partly for his own enjoyment, feeling the tight, thin walls clamp down on him and draw him further inside her.

He also needed to smooth the cream around as much of her inner entry as possible. They knew it would ease and speed up the healing process, so they could both enjoy his cock's penetration sooner.

As Kyli gasped and jerked her hips back, seeking a deeper penetration than what he already gave her, Max felt his own desires increase. He lowered his other hand to rest on her clit.

"Is this what you want?" he asked darkly, knowing the dominant tone of his voice and actions would turn her on even more.

"Kyli?" he checked, insisting on a response, refusing even the small satisfaction of him stroking her clit until she answered him.

"Yes!" she gasped, panting and throwing her hips back into his possession. "Yes, Max! I want you to touch me, to stroke me!"

"Then relax your ass, baby," he said, slowly starting to stroke her clit as his fingers moved even deeper into her ass. "This is *my* ass, I can't wait to plunge myself balls deep into it, to hold both your hips in my hands and to push myself as far as possible inside you. And do you know what I'll do then?" he teased, drawing out the moment.

Kyli had her head down, her back arched and her ass pushed as far back against him as she could. She embraced his words and every thrust of his action. She moaned and begged him for more with every move of her delicious body.

"Then," he said softly, "I will shoot my load so deeply inside you, you'll feel it up to your throat. You'll feel my cock inside your ass even when it isn't there. You'll wish for it every moment of the day and night and never feel complete without me."

With that, desperate to enact the scene he had just described, to shove his cock so far inside her they would fuse together, he tweaked her clit carefully and relished her deep scream of completion.

When her thighs trembled, shook from the force of her release, Max withdrew his fingers from her ass, wiped them carelessly on his own shirt and let Kyli fall stomach-down onto the big bed.

He stood and pulled off the shirt, letting it crumple to the floor.

Sitting back down, he pulled Kyli's lower half onto his lap.

"Ever had a spanking, darling?" he teased, feeling his cock swell even more at the thought. He lowered one hand to her pale cheeks. Caressing them gently, sensitively, he looked at her upturned face.

Her blue eyes sparkled, lust and a deep, dark understanding inside them. He knew instinctively she would be creamy and wet if he touched between her lips. Not letting his dark gaze stray from hers, he gently manipulated the position she lay in, to give him the best access to her.

He wanted to give her more pleasure than any other man, to bind her to him through every sexual way he possibly could. With another, last, caress, he smiled down at her.

"Brace yourself, my love."

With a careful, steady *whack*, he slapped her ass with his open palm. Noting the tiny, pale flush of red on her cheeks, he delivered three, then four more slaps to each ass cheek.

"You've been a naughty little girl, Kyli," he said, lust making him have to work for his voice. "Seven years, you made me wait for you. Seven long," *whack*, "hard," *whack*, "years!"

Feeling the heat radiate from her ass, he stopped. Paused a moment to breath deeply. Get some oxygen into his system and try to cool the almost boiling heat in his pants.

Gently dipping one finger past her lips, he found a veritable river flowing from her pussy.

"Ah, naughty little Kyli," he murmured, "I do believe that just turned you on even more. Made you more sensitive in your ass, didn't it? I bet it's made you burn and ache for me here."

Gently, reverently, Max turned her so she knelt on the floor between his spread legs. Her face was level with his and she had never looked more beautiful to him.

"Your face is flushed, Kyli. Your pupils are dilated and your pussy is dripping down to your knees."

"That was—"she huskily cleared her throat, "That was...amazing, Max. How did you know the right force? When to stop and pause, and when to speak?"

"Why darling," he leaned forwards, so their breaths mingled intimately, "I know *you*. I have spent many a night imagining your responses, thinking about you. And the few nights I wasn't plotting how to best punish you for leaving me all alone, I was asking prying, personal questions from Gregor."

He kissed her to stop her from talking. He didn't want to talk anymore. He wanted to thrust himself inside her. Yet he knew the cream hadn't had enough time to stop it from being too painful for her. He knew she wanted some pain, but he needed to give her more time.

As she moaned and writhed against him, crushing her breasts into his chest, he knew he needed to do something so neither of them would plead for actions they would regret. He didn't want to push Kyli enough that she begged him to ream her—it would cause her more pain later.

Yet he needed some relief, needed to feel her around him before he exploded from the intensity of his feelings for her.

The classic holo-bulb flashed in his mind. He had the perfect solution.

Sucking Kyli's tongue into his mouth, watching her eyes widen impressively with her feeling of being trapped, both in his mouth and between his legs, he paused, holding them both there for a second.

When he released her tongue, he pulled back slightly.

"There," he said softly, wanting the rumbling lust in his chest to quiet a little. "Now that I've got the taste of you on my lips again, I think you need to do something for me."

The cocky grin came back in a flash.

"I thought I had already done plenty for you."

"You're the one wet and creaming, my dear. Whereas I am as hard as the proverbial bar of iron."

To prove his point, he half stood, keeping Kyli trapped between his legs. With a quick, efficient flick of his wrist, he untied his pants and let them drop to his ankles. Sitting back down on the bed, he freed his legs and wrapped Kyli closer to him, locking his naked legs around her waist and drawing her even closer.

He loved the way her eyes widened at the immense, red-purple head of his shaft. He had never needed a woman more, never needed to plunge himself and sate his desires in one, very particular woman.

Gently, giving her plenty of time to squirm out from under his hand, he pressed her head down, down, down until she drew level with his thick, throbbing head. Without even waiting for his command, she opened her mouth and covered him in her wet heat.

Max moaned, his head falling back. She felt so wet, so warm and so close around his shaft it took him considerable effort not to start shooting immediately.

"Suck me off, baby," he moaned as he lost himself inside her. "Suck me until I come."

# Chapter Eight

Kyli sucked hard, creating a vacuum in her mouth. The warm, salty taste, unmistakably Max, filled her mouth and tasted better than ambrosia.

Kyli lifted her hands to clasp the length of Max's cock she couldn't fit into her mouth. Holding it firmly, she raised her head, until just the tip of him lay in her mouth. She ran the length of her tongue over the heated, plum-shaped head.

When Max groaned, began to fist her hair and gently press her head further down onto him she smiled around the immense shaft. He was big, thick and so delicious she couldn't help but suck him harder. If it wouldn't be a crime against female everywhere, she's want to eat him whole.

"Oh, yeah, baby," he moaned, obviously lost in his own world of pleasure, "suck me harder, deeper."

Happily, she complied. There was just something about following orders from this man that made her feel so feminine, so *sexy*.

Often, when she was out in the field as a merc, orders were very logical, something she would have done under her own steam anyway. At other times they were a pain in the ass, and made her grit her teeth and search ways to comply, yet it a way that would make her happy, satisfied.

Sexual orders from Gregor, in her past, had often been shocking, but always pleasurable. Orders from Max seemed like they would be just as luscious, just as devastatingly decadent. While she might fight and argue with him outside of the bedroom, she knew sexually, she would love following Max's orders.

Kyli lowered her head, swallowing as much of Max as she could bear. Loosening her throat, she pushed herself until she could feel the warm head touch the back of her throat.

She rubbed the skin down the base of his shaft, cupping his balls with her other hand. As she raised her head, sucking fiercely on his shaft, running her tongue along the length and around the tip, she gently rolled the heavy sacs of his balls.

"I want you to swallow, baby," Max said, his voice gravelly and hoarse with his need. Obviously he wouldn't be lasting much longer. Kyli smiled, glad and eager to see how she could drive Max just as wild as he could push her.

"Here it comes, Kyli, goddess, you're so good and hot!"

Kyli braced her knees apart as Max's thrusts came harder, lifting them both up from the bed. Max cried out, an animal, instinctive response to the fierceness of his release.

Kyli could feel the explosions as his sacs rose even more tightly, as his cock began to shoot his come straight down her throat. She lapped at every morsel, his seed hot, creamy and salty.

Finally, she could hear his breathing return to normal. Max fell back onto the bed as his legs relaxed and his muscles became softer. Cheekily, she continued to lick and suck a moment, keeping his cock in her mouth. She wanted him to really feel the loss of warmth her movement would create.

Slowly, she raised her head, sucking and tickling his shaft with her tongue as she did so. With a wet, sexy *pop* she disconnected with him, and lifted her face to smile into his eyes.

Her lover looked sated. A lazy, very satisfied cat who had drunk the cream. She snickered, giggling childishly as she realized, *no, it had been she to drink the cream!*

Max's large, warm hand cupped her face, raising her so she sat next to him on the bed. Lazily, he pulled them together, a tangle of arms and legs and warm skin. He kissed her, his lips soft and warm and almost drowsy.

After a moment, with plenty of licks and nibbles, he pulled back.

"What were you giggling at?" he asked, his voice still low and rough from his passion.

"Oh," she smiled, feeling carefree and impish as she hadn't since wet training, "Just puns, which one of us looked more like a cat who drank cream, until I realized that *had* to be me."

"Ah," Max smiled and Kyli relished the twinkle in his eye, "I'm not opposed to a measure of cream myself, though I do prefer going to the pot for it myself."

Kyli rolled to her side, laughing. She tried to swallow the laughs as Max followed her to his side, but she felt so happy, so light, she couldn't. She turned and wrapped her arms around her lover, feeling a deep satisfaction she had never experienced before.

When Max lay beside her, his arms cocooning them from the rest of the world, she felt as if she would never move, never leave the safety of the here and now.

Drowsily, she felt her eyes begin to close.

"Let's nap," Max suggested, "We can call Gregor later and find out what he knows about this Remington deal."

Happily, Kyli snuggled into her man. She would take him off guard next time, she promised herself, think of something so erotic he would simply die from a screaming, heart pounding orgasm.

With a huge smile on her face, she fell asleep dreaming of what would come.

# Chapter Nine

Kyli could feel a heated stretching in her ass. The pleasure could only be a deliciously erotic dream, she knew. It seemed to hover just out of her grasp. She felt full, an erotic pulling so intimate and sensual she thought she would burst.

Then she realized she was awake and on her stomach, Max's warm body pressed against her back and legs.

"Wakey, wakey, Kyli," he teased, his hot breath scorching her ear. "Time for me to ream this delicious ass of yours," he said, making her pussy cream with desire.

"Max," she said thickly, needing to clear her throat. "How many fingers?" she managed to say.

The dark, husky chuckle he answered her with made her long to turn around and pull him inside her.

"You barely even moved for my first finger, a waste of good lube," he said between nibbling her shoulder.

"The second," he continued, she couldn't help her shudder as he reached around her stomach and began to stroke her clit, "You moaned for, and restlessly moved your legs. Luckily for you, you called out my name in your sleep, or I'd have had to move straight onto the third."

Now fully awake, Kyli could feel the third finger in her ass, stroking away with the other two.

"Now, when I added my third with the first two, you jerked awake, and moaned so deliciously I'm having a hard time not to just ream you here and now."

"Max," she panted, unable to think what she wanted to say. She felt so full, so electrically aware of every inch of her flesh. She wanted to explode, to scream to the heavens and let her heart beat out of her chest.

Instead, she felt Max stroking her clit, building her orgasm inside her until she knew she had to scream just to release some of the tension.

"I think," she whispered, "I'm about to come."

"Come away then, baby," he replied easily, "and blow your mind. I know watching you come blows mine."

She closed her eyes, felt her back arch of its own volition. Lightning sensations zinged through her and she felt her pussy contract. She cried out, desperately wishing Max's thick length was inside her.

"Max!" she screamed again, unable to help herself.

"Oh, yeah, baby. I think you're ready for me now."

Hard on the heels of her climax she felt Max raise her onto her knees. Her head hung down, touching the pillow. In quick succession she felt him remove his fingers, causing her to groan with the loss, and then spread her cheeks wide.

"Max," she whimpered, desperately craving his penetration.

"Right here, baby," he softly answered her. She felt the hot head of his cock rest at her passage. In one delicious, fierce thrust he pressed deeply inside her.

"I'm right here, exactly where I've wanted to be for a long time."

"Oh, goddess," she moaned. She felt so incredibly full, so helpless under his penetration. Her ass felt like it was on fire, indescribable pleasure mingled with an aching fullness that bordered on true pain.

She felt Max draw back a few inches and she opened her mouth. She couldn't tell if she wanted to stop him or cry out from the pain from his movement.

Pleasure warred with pain in the manner she loved, coveted, but couldn't understand. And then Max thrust deeply back inside her, until she could feel his flat stomach pressing against the curve of her butt.

"You," he started, panting and gripping her hips so tightly she knew she'd have marks afterwards, "are so fucking hot, I don't know how I waited this long to ream you."

She could only moan and press back further onto him. His thickness, his length hurt, burnt the inside of her, but she desperately wanted more. More of him and the friction and fullness he could give her.

"Your muscles are clamping down on me, Kyli. I can feel you sucking the life out of me. If you want my soul, darling," he purred into her ear, tempting her beyond measure, "you're going to have to take it from me."

"No problem," she panted, resting her weight on one arm, reaching back with the other to grab his ass.

With all her might, with every ounce of strength she could give, she pressed him closer into her.

"I thought you were going to ream me, Max? Here I am, spread and penetrated, and yet I'm not screaming. What happened to making me unable to waddle, let alone walk?"

Knowing her taunting would only bring them both closer to the edge, she wiggled her hips at him. When he pulled back and then pressed back in she took a deep breath. Kyli closed her eyes and let the sensations wash over her.

Max had bent over her, so he nibbled on her neck, which she had unknowingly bared to him. One of his hands stroked her clit, making her crazy with the need to climax. His other hand held her hip steady, letting him get the best angle for them both, as well as letting him press into her. Hard.

"This is my ass," he repeated to her. "My woman. My ass. My Kyli."

Shocked, Kyli removed her hand. She hadn't known she had been digging her nails into his ass, pulling him further into her, wanting him as close as possible.

She felt all the blood rush from her head, her nipples ached, and so she took them into her own hands. She couldn't help herself, as soon as she pinched the erect tips, she could feel the detonation inside her begin.

Her clit throbbed as Max stroked it, plucked at it. Her nipples ached from how tight they were, not even her own grasping fingers could help assuage the need. Her pussy clenched. And her ass...her ass burned and felt so full she knew she would never forget this moment, never forget the feel of having Max inside her to the balls, pumping away at her.

"You better be ready to come, my love," Max said, "'Cos I think I'm about to blow my wad in this gorgeous, tight hole of yours."

His rough words toppled onto everything else. Kyli felt everything seize up, and she screamed as she came. The world tilted and receded. She couldn't hear, couldn't breathe, couldn't seem to do anything. All she could do was feel. The electric pulses in her pussy, the aching throb of her clit. And her lover pressing her hips into the bed as he pumped himself into her ass, shooting his seed deep inside her body.

They lay there on the bed, her on her stomach, him draped over her body for what felt simultaneously like forever and only a second. She moaned as Max lifted his weight away from her body and pulled his cock out from her.

He touched her so tenderly, so carefully, she felt emotion well inside her. She rubbed her face into the mattress so he wouldn't see the tears that formed in her eyes.

"I'm fine, Max," she said softly, her voice hoarse from all her screaming.

"I think I'll put some more healing cream inside you just to be sure. I'm sorry I couldn't resist and hold off for a day or so. I really don't want to hurt you."

Kyli smiled. Even if she had thought for a moment Max wanted to hurt her, she would have known he'd make her love it first.

"Honestly Max, I'm fine. I promise. A tad tender, but I loved it, wouldn't have missed it for all the stars in the galaxy."

She felt the bed dip as Max got up. She turned her head, too lethargic, too sated to be bothered with moving. Maybe she'd move in a year or so. She watched Max pick up the tube of healing cream and squirt a healthy amount onto his finger. As he dropped the tube back onto the floor, he picked up a face cloth from the bedside table as he climbed back onto the bed.

"Even so, I want you to lie here with me. We can nap again and get something to eat later. I know it's damn close to lunchtime, but I think we could both do with some rest."

Kyli smiled.

"Sounds just fine to me, Max. I need my quota of cuddling. I'd love to snuggle up to your body, and fall asleep."

Kyli felt her breath catch at the beauty of his smile. He was so darn handsome! He took her breath away.

"But first, darling, open up for me."

Considering how possessive, how masculine he had been while reaming her ass not two minutes ago, Kyli felt amazed at how gently, how reverently he touched her. One hand gently held her cheeks separate. The other hand eased itself inside her.

The cream felt cool, smooth. Strange how she hadn't noticed that earlier. Max gently smoothed it around her insides and then removed his finger. She was thrilled to see his seed mixed with the remnants of the cream. He squeezed more of the healing cream on and returned his fingers to her ass.

He then alternately wiped his seed with the cloth and placed more of the healing cream in her ass. Kyli couldn't help but smile at his tenderness, the obvious caring in his touch, which reflected in his face as he watched her.

When he had finished, Kyli moved to curl up on her side. She watched Max enter the bathing chamber to wash the cloth and his hands, clean himself with another cloth, and return to her, switching off the light sources on his way back.

He pulled the covers up and snuggled next to her, drawing her into his embrace.

"I'll make us something nice for lunch when we wake up. But for now, close those beautiful eyes of yours, or we'll both be too exhausted to make that trip out to Randor."

Kyli smiled and threaded her legs through Max's. She felt so sated, so relaxed and sexually satisfied she barely even noticed as she drifted off into sleep.

# Chapter Ten

Resisting the impulse to once again wake up his love, Max found himself carefully climbing out of his bed. He could hardly believe this happened to be the second time *today* he had to drag himself away from Kyli's sleeping seductiveness.

The few times he had taken lovers in the last few years, he had easily been able to fuck them raw and then push them to leave his bed. There had never been even a hint of this wistfulness, this craving for more and more.

He found it immensely amusing it didn't seem to matter how many times he plunged himself into Kyli, pussy *or* ass, he couldn't help wanting to start all over again as soon as he had shot his load inside her.

Tempting as she might be, he found it incredibly difficult to rise from the sex-scented sheets and head towards the shower stall. Glancing back at his sleeping love, he drank in the sight.

Kylie lay on her back, sprawled wide with only the thin navy sheet covering her delicious body. Her dark curls spread over the pillow and seemed to frame her sleeping face. He wished for a split second she were awake, that he could see her laughing blue eyes as he perused her beauty.

Yet he *really* needed to get moving. More than half the day had passed, and while Gregor fully understood what he and Kyli were doing, it still wasn't an excuse to ditch his responsibilities.

Stifling his sigh, Max privately admitted his duties had never seemed onerous before. He padded barefoot into the bathing chamber, mentally trying to get into his "work" mode.

Starting the water, adjusting the temperature, he waited until he had everything just the way he enjoyed it, and then stepped into the stall. Letting the hot water pound down onto his broad shoulders he took a deep breath and slowly let it out. Starting the reflection breathing exercises he had learned in his time out in the field, he began to cleanse his mind as well as his body.

When he could feel the pure air all the way through his chest and deep into his diaphragm, he let himself smile. He twisted his body, enjoying the easy flexibility he often took for granted. His mind clear, he enjoyed the fluid motion of his body and muscles as he picked up his vial of cleansing solution.

Max poured a small amount of the masculine scented solution into his palm and rubbed the lotion into his upper body. He felt a momentary pang to be ridding his body of the scent of Kyli. The pang turned into a grin when he realized after his shower he could wake his woman and, while they didn't have time to play, he could still retain her scent on his body.

Smiling, thinking about the different ways he could wake Kyli up, he felt a jolt of surprise when he heard the stall door click open. His hand automatically shot out to grasp whomever had snuck up on him, until he saw Kyli's smiling face.

"Goddess! Don't do that. I can't get rid of my fighting instincts, baby."

He couldn't help but smile as Kyli grinned back at him and shoved at him to make room for herself in the stall.

"Shove over, Max. And you're not the only one with fighting instincts. I think we have thoroughly concluded I won't break under a bit of pressure."

Max opened his mouth to argue the point, that *he* could certainly do more damage to *her* out of the two of them. Yet when she idly grabbed his cleaning solution and began to spread a small amount over her chest and stomach, he felt his breath hitch.

He could hardly believe it, but there seemed something so *intimate* about his lover, about *Kyli*, spreading his cleansing lotion over her own smooth, slick body. It looked and just felt so intimate, so sensual he couldn't help the hardening of his cock.

He half turned, so most of his back was to Kyli. He had spent the last five minutes thinking about getting to work and *not* awakening Kyli, now was not the time to get distracted.

"We need to comm Gregor, find out whatever he's been able to establish and probably pack to head off-world. You realize Im'an Remington isn't the star-tooth fairy? We'll need to be fast and discreet."

He watched as Kyli ducked her head under the spray, scrubbing at her hair and chuckling. The low, husky sound slid inside him, touching him in places deep inside he had never felt warm in.

"He is one of the leading helpers to the old regime — or maybe I should say *was*, the fight had all but ended when I left—he certainly wasn't Mr. Nice Guy. Yet if he is some kind of gun smuggler, it would make perfect sense. The Rebels had been planning for years, part of their attack was the element of surprise. The old regime didn't know what hit them. They would have needed the best weapons and needed them immediately. Why not scout the black market for a dealer?"

Max nodded and rinsed his body under the spray. When Kyli snaked a hand out and held his shoulder, pulling him close, he felt his heart accelerate.

"Kyli," he grumbled warningly. He had no sense of control with her, and he knew they *really* couldn't afford to do this now.

"I know, we have to go, but surely a good-noontime kiss wouldn't go astray?"

Max groaned at the teasing sound in her voice. She would be the death of him!

In one swift movement, he knew if she touched him any more he would burst into flames and all his good intentions would disappear, he swung her around so he had her backed into the wall.

He couldn't help but press tightly against her body, couldn't help but glory in the feel of her slick skin against his own much harder and heated flesh.

He bent his head, teasing her as she constantly teased him. He let his lips hesitate over her own, hover over hers as he counted the seconds. He breathed in her breath, wanting her to wonder for a moment if he really *was* going to kiss her.

Then, all in a rush, he lowered his lips to hers. He pressed them together, melded their bodies from lips to thighs. His hands rested on her waist, pulled her up toward him, his mouth ate hungrily at her lips, drinking in her scent and taste. The water poured over the both of them, as if it helped mold them together.

Feeling each breath positively burn in his lungs, Max began to reluctantly pull himself away. Slowly, inch by inch and relishing the way Kyli clung to him, he stood upright in the stall.

Looking down at her, knowing his gaze burned with the unrequited heat that zinged through his system, Max firmly gathered his control. He was not some horny wet-recruit anymore, he had grown into a man who could control his impulses and think clearly.

*Yeah, right,* his brain interjected, *And you're not dying to slam her up against the wall and thrust yourself balls deep inside her until you both come all over again.*

"We have to comm Gregor," he said, more to remind himself than her. Kyli smiled, making his heart feel light, and turned her back to him.

"You'd better get dried and dressed then. At the moment you simply scream 'I've-been-having-heart-pounding-screaming-sex-all-morning' and I don't think that's the impression you want to give Gregor when you make that call. I'll just finish here and be out in a sec."

Max shook his head and stepped out of the stall. Drying himself quickly, he stepped back into his bedroom and opened the windows to air the place out. Pulling on pants and shirt, he stripped the bed, resolving to make it up fresh later.

Sitting on the bare bed, hair still dripping slightly, he commed his oldest friend.

"Took you long enough," Gregor growled before he could even start his greeting, "you so owe me for all this.

Orders seem to be from On High we have to drop this. I explained about the investigation and the new data, and they said the case would be re-opened once Delta Force was finished with their Xefron Insurrection."

Max snorted.

"Which anyone with half a brain would realize won't be any time this century. So Kyli and I are heading in? Do you know where he is?"

"Two days ago, just like Kyli said, he was on Randor helping out the regime. There still aren't any reports back as to what's happened over there. All communications from there are down. It's only a few hours flight, so might be easiest to head on over. Particularly since Kyli already has the contacts over there."

Gregor ran a hand through his hair on the small screen. The dark circles under his eyes clearly stated the lack of sleep from last night.

"You look like shit, bro, you going to head home for a nap?"

Gregor snorted, laughter lighting his silver eyes for a moment.

"I wish. Some of us have to do the background work so your ass won't get fried over there. The basic information I've been able to find is Im'an's father has never been in the picture. Don't even know yet who he is. His mother met Am'ah's father while still pregnant with Im'an. They conceived Am'ah almost as soon as Im'an was born, and that's how they are so close together in age. They both seem to take after their mother looks-wise. I'll catch up with you tonight, hopefully with more data. So dish the news, you got lucky again, didn't you?"

Max smiled.

"Well, some of us are just born lucky—"

"And some don't know when to shut the hell up," Kyli interjected, hitting him on the shoulder. She grabbed the communicator from him and pushed him onto the mattress.

"Gregor, how do we know Remington's still on Randor if there's no communications from there?"

"We don't," he replied easily, "but even if the Rebels have rid themselves of the regime, it'd be very hard to just hop a starship and head on out. Ports were surely the first things they secured?"

Max rubbed his shoulder, which ached, and tried to effect a scowl. Kyli didn't even blink at him. Instead, she seemed totally focused on Gregor and the comm unit.

"Yeah." She answered his question, "that was mid last week. Okay, we can head on out right away. Keep us posted?"

"Of course," he purred huskily, teasing her and making her smile. Max didn't even feel a pang of jealousy. Really, he was getting the hang of this relationship business. As Kyli shut down the unit, he took it from her and stood up from the bed.

Picking up his work satchel and dropping the unit into it, he headed towards the door to get his shoes and socks.

"Do you need to bring anything?" he asked idly, his mind on the job ahead.

"Oh, we can just pick up my bag on the way through to the Port, it's on the way and I always keep one packed, not that I've really even *unpacked* yet. Are we heading out now?" she replied easily, following him out the door.

Later, Max would realize the casual manner in which she spoke always meant trouble, but with his mind firmly set on Remington and Randor, he didn't notice.

"Yep. Let's head on out, baby."

Five minutes later they were locking up the residence and heading towards his Cruiser and the Port to leave for Randor.

# Chapter Eleven

Kyli felt the most bizarre sense of déjà vu as she looked out the front of the small starship she and Max had borrowed. Touching the controls lovingly, she promised herself with her merc days behind her, she would soon arrange to buy a light beauty just like this.

The starship was compact considering the bulk some of the carriers that were around nowadays, yet its strength was only just slightly less than that of the much, much larger ships.

Kyli knew she wanted to stay in one spot, set down some roots and try to make a home for herself, but who could say when she would have a gut-full of working with the Force? Or want a few days cruising the stars, just to clear her head?

Now she no longer had a job in the "extremely high risk" category she could afford to get a loan big enough for a ship and not be paying the interest rates for the rest of her life. Banks were such blood sucking, evil creatures and credit loaners were worse, a breed only slightly above the criminal element. Some things never changed, no matter the date or place you were in the galaxy.

"You looking into making a purchase, baby?"

Kyli smiled. Max might have his eyes and mind firmly on the field ahead, might be starting the landing procedures as Randor became larger and larger, yet he still could notice her gentle caressing of the instruments in front of her.

Chuckling, she brought her hand back and re-snapped her safety belt. Paying more attention to the comm screen in front of her, she decided to shotgun his landing efforts.

"You could say that. Now I'm not a merc I'll get a loan much easier. I had thought to be buying a residence, but I think I'll get more pleasure out of a little starship like this. Get away every now and then on the weekends, or when I start feeling claustrophobic in the city main."

She wondered at the solemn nodding from Max. It wasn't that she didn't expect him to understand, but more as if he had already thought about it. Why must the man always be a step ahead of her? She thought about the bag she had left in the Temple of Lights with one of her closest friends. Maybe for once she could be a step ahead of him this next time.

Smiling secretly to herself, she didn't realize Max was watching her so closely until he leaned over the small gap between them in the control room. He cupped her face and turned her towards him.

"What are you smiling at, baby? You got secrets still?"

She laughed outright at these words.

"Always! A girl has to keep her man on his toes, doesn't she? Besides, admit it, you'd be bored senseless if I didn't have a few more cards up my sleeves." She continued to chuckle as he shook his head in masculine pride and annoyance.

"You're going to turn me gray long before my time."

Kyli took one look up and down his impressive physique, his dark skin, so smooth and perfect. Her eyes lingered on his short, curly hair, as black as the night. The thought of turning him gray almost made her laugh aloud again.

With his gleaming dark eyes and pearly white teeth, Kylie knew she would age well before he began to show the effects of age upon his body. She couldn't help but snort in amusement.

"Yeah, right! I think a bit of healthy fear on your part would be a welcome addition to this budding relationship."

The hand that cupped her face started to stroke down her neck, it sent tiny shots of feeling to her breasts and pussy. She bit her lip to stop a moan from escaping.

"You don't need to try, baby," he reassured her, "you keep me excited and entertained enough just by being with me. Whatever little surprise you're cooking up can just wait until we return home."

Kyli laughed as the console started to beep at him. Swearing, Max returned his attention, and unfortunately for her, his hands, to the ship and the flickering switches as he prepared to land at Randor Major.

# Chapter Twelve
*Randor Major — the newly conquered City Main.*

"You tired of your hometown lifestyle already, my girl?"

Kyli turned as she and Max finished paying the young-looking cadet to watch over their starship, to greet the large, crinkled brow of one of her most loved friends.

"Sandar!" she cried out, rushing to hug the elderly man. He returned the embrace just as tightly. She grinned to think how they must look.

Less than forty-eight hours had passed since they had seen each other last, yet when they had parted, they hadn't been sure when they would next meet up. Seeing her again so soon was obviously a shock to the man, but a good one.

"Sandar, this is a friend of mine, Max," she started to introduce as she pulled away.

"Got eyes, don't I, girl? Nice to see you took my advice and found a decent man to fuck. You deserve it."

"Umm," she felt her face heat slightly at her old friend's blunt words. *She* didn't mind her friend had been telling her for most of her last campaign to get herself laid, but she felt strange having him say so right here in front of Max and half the Port.

Despite his earthy words, the men seemed to like each other on sight. Max took a step forward with a grin and his hand outstretched. He thankfully waited while Sandar looked him over approvingly and also reached out to shake the proffered hand.

Kyli smiled and shook her head. She was used to the man's rough, blunt ways, but it still came as a surprise when he voiced his earthy opinions in front of strangers, and even more of a surprise Max didn't seem to mind in the slightest. In fact, he seemed rather approving of the old man and his thoughts.

"What you bringing my girl back here for? Job's over. Llelo stormed what remained of the old regime's castles early yesterday morning, finished with them and their supporters. He's been working on the cleaning up since then. We'll all be right as rain in a few weeks and can all get back to business."

Kyli hugged the old man again, pleased everything had worked for him and their friends.

"Do you know where Am'ah and Im'an Remington are?"

The old man pushed his hat back and stared at her. She resisted the impulse to fidget. It seemed as if Sandar knew of the two Remington brothers and didn't want her involved.

"Am'ah and Im'an Remington," he repeated carefully. Kyli looked him in his pale blue eyes and held her ground. Sandar had been her friend all these long months she had been working and consulting on her last job. They had spent so much time together they knew each other better than they would their own family.

Sandar had become like a father, grandfather and overprotective brother to her, all rolled up into the one feisty, crusty old man. When he turned to Max, she winced, knowing what was to come.

"What the three hells you doing taking my Kyli to follow those two riff-raff? She's supposed to be starting her new life, settling down, not following up on old business!"

As he took a breath and Kyli noticed the thin blue veins in his hands begin to plump up, she decided discretion truly could be the better part of valor.

Taking his hand, distracting him, she turned to move him aside so she could try to gain some privacy. There wasn't much to be afforded in the large starship hanger, but she felt certain she could find a spot away from Max and the obvious argument about to ensue.

"Sandar, I need to talk to you in private a moment," she began, eyes wandering to a clear corner on the other side of the hanger.

"It's okay, Kyli. I think this is better man to man."

Kyli felt a spurt of surprise as Max gently removed her hand from Sandar's and led the old man a few paces away by gentle pressure on his shoulder.

When the elder man followed without a peep of trouble, Kyli moved further back. She scrambled in her bag for a moment and took out the sheets of paper she needed to get stamped. She had the paperwork for their ship in one hand to act as a cover while she grilled one of the younger helpers hanging around.

She knew full well both men could handle themselves, and knowing them as she did, she knew she only had five minutes to find out what she needed to know. "Hey!" she called out to a passing port-boy, flashing a few credits in front of him, "I've just returned, and I need you to confirm that the Temple of Light..."

* * * * *

"This is all rather easy, Mr. Sandar," Max began. He knew the old curmudgeon had only tried to protect Kyli. So he decided to explain, rather than rant. "A friend of mine and I work within the Force but also in our own investigations unit. Im'an Remington is thought to be a gun smuggler. We want to uncover a few things about him. Kyli and I go way back, and we hooked back up again last night. Unfortunately, when she found out I was investigating Remington, she decided to stick her two credits into the barrel."

Max paused as the old man snorted. "Sounds damn like my Kyli. So now you're chasing the two of 'em out here?"

Max nodded. "That's the plan."

The old man eyed him carefully. "So what's with you and my Kyli?"

Max smiled. Cross the galaxy, cross the millennium, and fathers were all the same. "I hope to settle down with her, preferably some day soon. Right now she's skittish so this relationship is a new beginning for us both. We parted on less than good terms a number of years ago but I hope to ease her into things, take things slowly and not scare her away."

The man looked at him, and then a small way across the hanger to where Kyli seemed to be talking to a port-boy about their ship's papers. Sandar cocked his head—as if to hear better?—and chuckled.

"You do that, son. My girl is just full of surprises."

Max blinked, wondered what had just happened, then shrugged the thought away. He turned back to Kyli, and noticed she made a few last gesticulations to the port-boy, caught him watching her and headed back their way. He felt pride and relief when she took his hand as she came up to his side.

She handed him their stamped papers and he put them away in his pack.

"Masculine chest-beating all out of the way?" she teased.

When Sandar nodded, Max noticed an odd glint in his eye.

"This one's a keeper, darling."

Max felt his face, unbelievably, flush as she nodded to the old man.

"I know. It's under control."

Max cleared his throat, uncertain with the feeling of things not being in his control. He couldn't help but think they knew something he didn't, and they hadn't even had to talk about it.

"So, the two Remington half brothers?" he started.

"Am'ah is in the lockup in the city main. Im'an is anyone's guess. Do you want to see Llelo first?" Sandar turned to Kyli.

Max let her think and make the decision. She knew the situation here better than he, so she could make the call. "Maybe on our way out. Let's see what Remington One can tell us first, so we can make our plans."

Nodding, Max retained a firm hold on her hand, not wanting to let her go. It was a strange, new sensation, but a wonderful one.

# Chapter Thirteen

Kyli enjoyed throwing Max off balance. She greeted people whom she knew, pointed out different bits and pieces of crumbling ruins and buildings that remained still standing. It felt odd, coming back here such a short time after leaving and never wanting to return. She held no bad memories here as such, this had just been her last assignment. One more for the road, so to speak.

She had made a few good friends in her months here, Sandar and a Priestess the best of them, but she held many more acquaintances. It took almost no effort at all to find out where Am'ah was being held, awaiting his sentencing.

As they came up to the sandstone building with only one young guard she didn't recognize, she smiled and showed him her merc pass.

"Oh yeah, Kyli, Thom commed me a minute ago to tell me you were on your way. I'm Jakob. He with you?"

The question, so easily put, made her smile wide. She knew Max was used to leading things, used to being in charge. She threw him a cheery grin over her shoulder.

Surprisingly, he didn't look sulky or even out of sorts with her being the lead. He looked solid, dependable, completely in control and happy to follow where she led. It made her feel all warm and gooey inside.

Blinking, she brought her attention back to focus. *Warm and gooey?* her mind repeated. *Since when do we feel warm and gooey over a man when we should be concentrating on work?*

Kyli mentally shrugged and pushed the new feelings, as well as the sarcastic mental thoughts to the back of her mind. "Yeah, we're here to talk to Remington. Is that okay?"

The solider shrugged and stepped aside to let them enter. "Roald is inside. Just clear it through him."

Kyli smiled and stepped into the narrow building, knowing Max would follow her. Once they cleared the entryway she stopped and turned to him.

"What are we going to ask Am'ah when we get to him?" she asked softly, moving closer to allow the small flow of traffic to move around them.

"Do you trust me to lead that bit?" Max replied quietly.

"Of course," she insisted. "I just don't want to walk in blind. Are we playing good merc–bad merc, or something else? I don't want to have to second guess what you're doing."

Max smiled, his charming, roguish grin that would do the best space pirate proud. "I honestly have no idea. I'll let you know when I think of it."

Kyli rolled her eyes, well used to Max's off-the-cuff style approach. "Goddess give me strength. It'll be a Plan C all over again, right?"

They both chuckled as they headed towards the main office area. Plan C was always what their wet team had privately qualified as "anything goes to get the job done", otherwise known as they didn't have a clue and were making it up as they went along.

Many of the training programs they had worked through insisted they list their plans ahead of the game. Plan C usually consisted of the description Top Secret, meaning no details needed to be given ahead of time. They reverted back to it whenever nothing went according to plan and they had to fudge their way through the mission. Surprisingly enough, it usually worked with the Management.

Kyli couldn't help the thrill of excitement entering her system at the thought of working with Max again much like their younger days.

They passed through open doors and by two guards keeping watch. Kyli started to show her pass, but Roald stood up and greeted her warmly enough that the guards immediately went back into position at the door.

"Kyli! Good to see you. I heard you were back."

Kyli stepped forward to greet the tall, balding man. Roald was far taller than her, and built like the proverbial outhouse. He had left a few scars from various fights simply for the look of being tough and rugged, yet the sheer size of his muscled bulk often gave more than enough intimidation. She had never seen him have to do more than raise his voice, so powerful was his presence and reputation.

After the rather messy war, Kyli had the feeling Roa could keep order on Randor from sheer reputation al But time would tell.

"Of course you heard I was back on site. Ev always comms you first."

"Must be my handsome good looks," h shaking hands warmly with her. "I heard you a wanted to talk to Am'ah. Anything I sho involved in?" At this, Kyli took a half step back and let Max take over.

"Max Thonkins, Special Armed Forces. First up, I really haven't come here to step on toes. My partner and I have been watching Im'an for a number of months. Intel didn't even mention his half-brother and the case seems to have been squashed. We're uncertain why, or more likely, who's being paid to bury the case. I simply would like to talk to Am'ah and see what I can find."

Kyli smiled slightly. Lovely to see Max's diplomacy skills hadn't become rusty in the intervening years. Amazing really.

"Well, I have no problems with that. We're keeping communications closed by and large. The old regime had so many tentacles everywhere the best bet, we feel, is to simply get rid of as many snags as possible while everything can be declared 'such a mess', and then we'll be able to start from there. Llelo and I agree on that. We both feel it would be best to clean up as much as possible while we can be diplomatic and keep everyone, the Force included, out of our business. You will tell me if you find something you think would be useful to our situation?"

"Of course," Max agreed, knowing more than likely would surreptitiously listen in on their anyway. But it still made sense to reassure

" Roald led them through another mall holding room. Max politely mander's fingerprint, eye scan entered into the screen to

Three men were being held in separate partitions. Roald briefly looked over all three partitions and then waved Max and Kyli into one of them. They both turned slightly as Roald closed the door behind them and resealed the laser system.

"Just holler when you're done, men," he said in his most commanding voice, exiting without giving any of the prisoners an idea of what was going on.

Kyli turned to watch Am'ah Remington. He sat with his back ramrod straight, pride and arrogance oozing from him as if he were on a throne and not in a cell. His blond good looks were enough for many women, the bright masculine beauty of an archangel.

Yet she could see below it, to the empty soul. Here was a man who didn't care whether he hurt, maimed, or killed. His eyes were a light brown, and seemed completely soulless to her. He might be physically gorgeous, but his eyes were dead in a way she had almost never seen. He was evil personified.

It felt strange. In Max and Gregor, their arrogance seemed to come from deep inside them. They *knew* they were good and weren't afraid to admit or believe it. Am'ah's arrogance only made him seem more sinister, more shallow a person somehow.

It almost felt as if somewhere deep inside himself he knew he had done despicable things and would do so again, so he couldn't have pride in himself like Max and Gregor could.

In fact, the more she looked at him, the more creeped-out she became. She had only experienced this once or twice before, but she could almost *feel* the ugliness clinging to his soul, to his inner self. She swallowed down the feeling of large, black hands coming out to touch her, to taint her soul.

The rare other times she had come across pure evil encased in a human body she had felt very similarly like this. She took a deep breath, trying to push aside her stupidity.

"Am'ah," Max greeted the man quietly and stood, patiently waiting.

Kyli watched warily as Am'ah raised his eyes to look over Max. The light brown eyes reflected no interest, no emotion. Kyli frowned. Often men caught up in the middle of a struggle would know others would come to bargain with them. Yet Am'ah didn't seem interested in the least.

"I do not need your aid," he stated emphatically, as if his words alone would send both her and Max scuttling back to where they came from. She could tell this man was used to saying something once and having everyone around him jump to obey.

His eyes moved on to Kyli, and she straightened her own spine. His gaze raked over her and she could feel her skin crawl. The feeling of black oil, or just sheer, unadulterated darkness enveloping her made her feel physically ill.

For one short moment she felt immensely grateful she had spent so many years training and being a merc. She knew how to hide her emotions, she knew how to clamp down heavily on her fear and revulsion and not let any of it show. She knew the silent breathing and meditation exercises to look impassive and wait out the disgusting feeling of being looked over like some animal.

It cost her all her will to not reflect anything of her revulsion or worry on her face, but she felt incredibly proud she managed to do it.

"Although," he said slowly dragging out the words ponderously, "I might well do with your...time." He finished with a sneer.

The darkness she had sensed in him was nothing compared to the thick black oily feel of his full and undivided attention. Now he actually looked at her, focused his will on her, she could barely function. She felt as if she were drowning in pure evil.

Kyli continued to stand where she was, taking slow, even, very deep breaths as she had trained herself to do when she felt uneasy or panicked. She imagined breathing in pure, light energy and air, drawing it all the way down into her belly and diaphragm. As the air passed down into her she felt it cleansing her, and as she slowly and softly exhaled, she imagined all the blackness of Am'ah's attention being exhaled in a smoky puff, pushing it outside of her pores and body. After she had done this a few times, staring at the evil man in front of her steadily, she felt far more relaxed and in control of herself.

Kyli strongly resisted the temptation to reach over and punch him out, to beat the shit out of him. A man as evil as he had to have done unmentionable things before, and worse, got away with it and so he made himself feel even more powerful. The more he got away with, the stronger his confidence, and quite possibly the more his cravings for doing such horrible things would increase.

Sadly, Kyli decided not to beat him as he deserved. Even though Am'ah might still look rakishly handsome with a broken nose and wired up jaw, with bruises all over his face and body, and even though she knew Roald would never press charges, they needed his help.

Kyli frowned slightly at her thought. *No, they didn't need his help, that would make him feel important and validated. His information,* she assured herself. They only needed some information out of his mind.

Kyli slowly came back to herself as she relaxed more. She could still feel the evil emanating from Am'ah, but she had it under control now. As she felt herself fall back more heavily into her body, the weight of Am'ah's stare diminished slightly. Kyli became far more attuned to Max, however. From the menace and seriously angry vibrations radiating from him, she could well believe *his* tolerance was waning.

Kyli chuckled softly. She had known how bad her own reaction to Am'ah had been, she could well imagine the possessive, annoyed reaction Max would have as he slowly realized just how badly Am'ah made her feel.

The serious interest and speculation in the evil man's eyes wouldn't help soothe Max's temper, either, she silently bet to herself. Not wanting to reach out and touch Max while in the presence of Am'ah, Kyli made do with stealing a glance and trying to reassure him with her eyes.

Max nodded his head curtly, flexing his hands. Kyli smiled to herself. He had been clenching them and she'd bet a number of credits they were feeling rather cramped now. As Am'ah seemed so interested in her, she decided to continue their questioning for Max.

"We're not here to offer you a deal," she started softly, wondering whether Am'ah would answer more questions with her soft and docile, or ball-buster Amazon-woman strong. "We're here to ask why there's so much pressure for your brother to be let off from his actions."

Am'ah shrugged, completely uninterested. "We have power," he stated simply.

Kyli frowned. The simple, unconcerned way he stated it made her skin crawl again. Kyli took anther deep breath of clean air to cast off her revulsion and help her concentrate more deeply on finding the clues and answers in his replies.

While many men before him had believed they held power, believed they were gods and all sorts of other things, none she had ever met had seemed so self-assured. His inner confidence was slightly revolting in that so much assurance in so evil a creature bespoke a man who had never been called to account for his actions.

The thought this particular man had never been held responsible for anything he did reminded Kyli why she had wanted to stay within the "upholding the Laws" industry. Men like this needed to be reckoned with and given a time of judgment.

Kyli smiled wryly. The "he's mad" theory didn't ring true either. Am'ah certainly didn't seem to be living in a fantasy world, didn't seem to be delusional. Kyli cocked her head to one side. Something niggled on the edge of her thoughts, something she had heard, or maybe read.

She knew with a hazy, unclear remembrance of talk about how the Remington brothers have their tentacles in every pie in the galaxy. Kyli shook her head in dismay. That knowledge didn't help her any! It didn't take a genius to notice that someone as arrogant as the man sitting casually in this jail cell wouldn't be satisfied unless he had a hand in every unspeakable act that occurred.

In fact, it would probably tickle his fancy to make damn sure he *did* have something to do with all the various acts of illegal activity throughout the galaxy. That thought led Kyli to the thought she knew she had been grasping for.

Am'ah must have friends in high enough places to know he had nothing to fear from higher reprisals. That would account for a large part of his arrogance and certainty, not to mention his confidence that nothing would hurt him.

"You think you're going to get out of here, don't you?" Kyli asked, unable to stop her thoughts. If he held a connection, almost any connection, to someone with power throughout the galaxy, it could explain a lot. Not only about how he came to be this unrestricted and evil, but also how the investigations into his half brother could be smothered back in the Force.

"I *know* I'm going to get out of here, woman. Take off your shirt," he said, lowering his voice in what she could only assume he thought of as sexy, or maybe commanding.

Unable to help herself she rolled her eyes and placed one hand on her hip. The action felt so automatic she couldn't have helped doing it even if she wanted to. The breathing exercises, not to mention the showing of feminine strength, of not submitting to him made her head clear even more. His presence still tainted the room, but she was resisting it more and more easily now.

"Oh please, I'm not some stupid teenager. Who are you connected to, and how?"

At her antagonism, he stiffened. His pale eyebrows raised slightly, in surprise, she knew. No way would this man feel fearful of *her*. Kyli couldn't help but smile more. He seemed as if he couldn't believe she had acted such to him. Outrage warred with a nasty temper. Here was one man, she decided, she didn't want to cross.

"I do not have to deal with this," he muttered nastily under his breath. "Bloody females, thinking they rule the world. Well I'll show all of you." He looked up and Kyli couldn't help herself, she raised an eyebrow mockingly.

Before she could tease or taunt him further, hoping to get something else from him, Am'ah had raised his voice. "Guards! Guards! Get rid of these intruders! They annoy me!"

Kyli shook her head and waited for Roald to return. Knowing Am'ah was dry, or would simply refuse to say anything more of any semblance of use, Kyli took a the few steps back so she could leave the tiny room as soon as Roald opened the locks. She ignored Max as he bent down to whisper in Am'ah's ear. She didn't even bother to turn around and try to work out what he was saying. Am'ah was a slimy little worm and she sincerely hoped he would rot in the three hells for eternity.

Roald couldn't unlock the systems fast enough for her. She walked ahead of Max, who stood up to follow her as Roald unlocked the door. Kyli kept her steps even and at a normal pace, determined not to break into a run.

As she walked down the long, thin corridor she shook her head and tried to wipe discreetly at her arms. She felt unclean after mere minutes in the man's presence.

Kyli continued to breathe deeply, trying to discern what made her feel all flighty and panicked about Am'ah. She certainly was no Seer, but she couldn't help the tiny thrill of panic in her mind. Was this man somehow going to hurt her? Or Max?

She headed back into Roald's main office and resisted the strong impulse to rub at her arms even more. She knew the atmosphere wasn't cold, but she could feel the slight chills shiver down her back. Kyli felt so unclean she desperately wished for a shower.

She turned around to face Roald as soon as he had the three of them back in his office. Not even waiting to be offered, she crossed over to the hidden cabinet door and brought out a bottle of Red Fire Whiskey. She delicately took a swig directly from the bottle.

The heated, molten fire ran down her throat and seemed to soothe everything across its path that it touched upon. Kyli closed her eyes, to better feel the burning liquid as it soothed her like no amount of meditative breathing exercises could. Taking a deep breath and letting it out in a whoosh, she replaced the cap, put it back in its "secret" hiding place and turned back to the boys.

They both stared at her, openmouthed and shocked beyond belief. Kyli raised an eyebrow in the eternal way of a woman.

*What?* she asked with her posture and gesture. Roald and Max exchanged a glance and simultaneously shrugged. Kyli smiled slightly as she realized neither man wanted to say anything.

Deciding a definite change of subject was being called for, she let herself flop down in one of the uncomfortable chairs.

"You are going to execute that creep, aren't you? I don't know how I know, but he's done some terrible, horrible things. He's as close to pure evil as I've ever come across."

Roald and Max looked at her for a moment. She couldn't tell from their looks anything they were thinking, and she felt like a bit of a freak.

"What?! You don't believe me?" she asked, wounded.

Roald cleared his throat, his face and hand gesture placating. "I *know* he's done awful things, Kyli. The problem is, the only thing he's said since his capture has been the name Rosdan Tredla."

Both she and Max froze.

Everyone across the galaxy knew Rosdan Tredla. He had taken over his first planet at eighteen. By twenty-five he had an entire army under his control and had never lost a battle. For over twenty years he had been the most bloodthirsty of all leaders. He wielded his power like an almighty war-axe, certain to chop anyone in his way into tiny pieces.

And then he had turned to politics.

All that power and ruthlessness had merely grown, not shrunk with his age. No one dared defy him. Those that had always ended up dead or much worse. If the two Remingtons had any connection with Rosdan Tredla then it came as no surprise the Force had been unable to squash the gun smuggling and any other misdeeds either brother performed.

In a strange way, Kyli felt the knowledge settle and gel completely with everything else she had gathered and learnt in the last few minutes. *This* would account for the uncanny knowledge that Am'ah had never been held accountable for his actions. No one very close to Tredla ever *would* be brought into line and made to take responsibility for his own crimes.

Hell, it would be quite likely such things would be rewarded, or applauded, rather than cast judgment over.

Rosdan Tredla might be old, infirm and in failing health. But while he still lived, anyone who crossed people he considered his own would be in major trouble.

"Do you know the connection?" Kyli asked, feeling a trifle worried. If Am'ah Remington truly was considered by Tredla to be under his protection, and word got out he had been murdered, then heads would roll. Literally.

In the back of her head the tiny kernel of an idea that had began to form died a quick death. Roald would be in incredible trouble if he were found to have executed, or even be implicated in murdering Remington in any way. And Tredla would find out, no doubt about that at all.

Kyli wondered if she could kill Remington herself. She looked into herself for a moment, and then cast the thought aside. She had been a merc for many years, yet she couldn't be sure she could murder a man in cold blood. Even one as evil as Remington.

"I've sent out feelers and have men trying to work on it, but it's early days yet. Not much has come back to me."

"Don't worry," Max reassured Roald. "We can find out. My partner is looking into it already. I'll just comm him with what we have."

Kyli didn't resist as Max took her elbow and led her from the room and back out into the sunshine. She blinked, felt for a moment as if she had been inside that cell for years, and not just the ten minutes it had been in reality.

"Max, what do we do now? The usual method of justice obviously isn't going to work well here. Besides, it's not like we can do anything to Tredla. He's far too well protected. Half the underworld has been trying to knock him off for over fifty years. I doubt we can do anything to him they haven't tried. "

Max shook his head and smiled tenderly down at her. Kyli felt her heart melt a little.

"My bloodthirsty little merc. I certainly wouldn't expect to try for Tredla. Besides, he's so old and infirm he won't last too many more years. He's suffering enough knowing large chunks of his dynasty will be divided up after his death. He never did appoint a successor early enough to train them. That in itself is a form of justice."

Kyli opened her mouth to argue, but Max hushed her by gently placing a finger over her mouth.

"First, we get ourselves a room and contact Gregor. Then we can try to work something out. But I still vote for going for Remington, not Tredla. Let's start here at the beginning, huh?"

Kyli nodded reluctantly and gently pulled her arm out from Max's grip. She took them down a side street and into a nicer area that hadn't been damaged as much by the fighting.

Grinning broadly, she led them both into a clean-looking bar with the sign "The One-Eyed Man" hanging over its door. "I thought it appropriate," she teased, looking at Max's impressive crotch. "I love a good one-eyed man."

Max slapped her on the ass, eliciting a startled yelp and a laugh from her. He strode up to the back of the bar and asked for a room. She couldn't help but admire his rear as he waited for the bartender to get the key.

The barman had lasergrams all over his arms, and probably in a number of other places as well. The all seemed to merge, one over another, making it difficult for Kyli to see what they all were in the dim light. Yet on one arm they all seemed to surround a naked woman giving fellatio to a snake.

*Interesting,* she privately acknowledged, but personally she preferred the view of Max's ass.

She followed Max a moment later to the back of the bar and down the hallway. The room looked clean and neat, definitely good enough for a night or two's stay.

Max had already dropped his bag beside the bed and pulled out his personal comm unit. Kyli dropped beside him, bouncing slightly on the bed.

"So what now, Mr. Special Armed Services?"

"We comm Gregor and then we wait," he replied easily, punching in the sequence to garner Gregor's attention.

# Chapter Fourteen

Max tried to hide his temper, but found it incredibly difficult. He didn't understand the particulars of the undercurrents he had been able to feel passing between that slime Am'ah Remington and Kyli. He had never felt so useless and helpless before, and hoped to heaven he never felt that way again.

He had been attuned enough to Kyli to understand her deep breathing, had been able to recognize the stress and tension in her body. Even though he had been standing in the same room as the two of them, it had been patently obvious Kyli had gathered more than he had.

Whatever had been happening, it had made her skin pale and clammy to the touch, and that made Max livid. Am'ah had made his baby feel awful and Max now felt the most bizarre combination of helplessness and anger. He had wanted to tear the man apart, piece by piece, but had thought himself noble in restraining his baser, more instinctive impulses.

If Am'ah really did have ties to Rosdan Tredla... Max shook the thought away before he could follow down *that* path anymore.

He had met so many men, good, bad and indifferent, he supposed he had created a bit of a shell around himself. Things that used to bother him no longer did.

Maybe Am'ah couldn't even tell how much he upset Kyli, and a large part of him hoped the bastard couldn't see the effect he had on her. Yet he knew her well enough, both physically, as well as emotionally from their past together, that he could easily tell he had upset her a lot.

His gut clenched. Am'ah was definitely one nasty character, a mean son-of-a-bitch who had obviously spent much of his life cultivating the sort of connections Max and Gregor spent their lives destroying.

It certainly wouldn't be a hardship to place a beamer between his eyes. Now he just had to work to make sure no one he knew or cared about was held responsible for it.

As much as he wanted to lay Kyli down on this bed, strip her naked and assure her of her safety in the oldest way known to man, he needed to get information fast.

Finally Gregor answered his comm. The tiny hologram of his disheveled face appeared. Hair mussed, some light stubble on his chin and jaw, the man looked a mess.

Unable to help himself, Max jeered at his friend. "You look like you're having yourself a bender. Are you attacking the Red Whiskey 'cos you miss me so badly?"

Gregor snorted. "Dammit, Max. You've forgotten the time changes, haven't you? It's an early hour of the morning for social calls, even for you. Some of us enjoy our beauty sleep at three in the morning."

Max snickered. He *had* forgotten the difference in the time, but it wouldn't have mattered one iota to him, even if he had remembered.

"Go dunk your head in a bucket. We've probably found the connection. Rosdan Tredla."

"No shit?" Max watched Gregor run a hand through his hair and come more awake by the second. "Tell me you're being cruel to annoy me."

"Do I look like I'm laughing, man?"

"Aw, fuckit. This is not what I want to hear at this hour. Talk to me."

Quickly and concisely he summarized their findings. As they both sat there in silence, pondering, Kyli added in her two credits.

"He's really evil, Gregor. I was there when we spoke to him." Max stroked her arm with his free hand as she shivered at the memory. "I mean really, really pure evil. Have you managed to dig up anything about him?"

Gregor nodded slowly, watching her every movement. Max knew his buddy. He was weighing things in his mind, analyzing something at a lightning speed. Max had a sneaky suspicion his buddy was trying to decide whether whatever information he needed to share would be too much for Kyli or not. Max also realized he didn't feel overly protective, or particularly upset at Gregor making this decision for them. The warrior in Max rebelled, but watching how even the memory of Remington affected his woman, he knew he'd stand by whatever rabbit Gregor pulled from his hat.

After a moment, Gregor smiled slightly and sent a wink to Kyli.

"Good to see you, sugar. Officially, no. There's not much at all in the Force records. I have a feeling everything about him and his half-brother routinely gets shredded and ditched, and only pure luck and a laxness in Management is the cause of this smuggling stuff coming to our attention.

"Unofficially, however, there's a truckload on him. I've hacked into a number of different areas and what these guys have done will give you nightmares for years.

There almost isn't any area of crime these two haven't had something to do with. If we're careful and think about it, I'm sure we can make it look like someone else has just taken advantage of the unrest over there."

Max watched Kyli nod solemnly, and then rest her gaze on her bag. He idly wondered if it was the beamer she carried in there, or something else that she thought about, but then Gregor recaptured his attention.

"Leave this to me. I'll do some hacking, find out what is really going on. Once we know that, I'll be able to work out a way for us all to deal with this. I'll also find out what exact connection Tredla has to Remington. We could be in deep shit here and so we'll have to tread lightly. Besides, chances are if Remington has been there, then Tredla has a shitload of contacts there, and you guys won't be able to discover anything without arousing suspicion. At least you guys won't be sleeping either…" he muttered as Max could hear him opening drawers and shuffling things.

"Night, Gregor," Kyli called out as she crossed the room, picked up her bag and headed for their small bathing chamber. When the door clicked closed behind her, Max turned again to his friend.

"I don't really understand how or why but that bastard really upset Kyli. Can you figure something out fast? I have a feeling things here are going to get explosive soon, and personally I want Kyli well away from the mess. See if you can figure a way for me to take him out without anyone noticing. The last thing we need is for Tredla to get wind of me murdering someone he has a strong connection to. That would not solve any of our problems."

Gregor nodded and ran a hand over his face. "You owe me for this buddy. And don't think I'll forget to collect. You owe me big."

Max nodded, understanding perfectly. "I hear you. Just holler when you need anything at all from me, bro."

With that, he shut down the unit and placed it back into its slot in his watch. Standing up from the bed, he cocked his head and listened. Sure enough he could hear the sound of the water running.

He pulled off his shirt, carelessly tossing it to the floor. Toeing off his shoes, he crossed the room to double check that the door was locked.

After pulling the spindly chair in front of the door to give them at least a warning if anyone should break into the room, he crossed back over to where his bag lay. Opening it, he removed his personal care pack and stripped off his socks and pants.

Smiling wickedly, he left his boxers on and pushed open the door to the bathing unit. Thin curls of steam rose from the unit, snatches of humming coming from under the spray. Max carefully closed the door, not wanting to alert Kyli to the fact he was creeping up behind her.

Pulling his boxers off, he carefully stepped into the cubicle and wrapped his arms around Kyli's waist. Taking another step forward, so his thigh came between her spread legs, he pressed them against the cold tile wall.

"Wanna play?" he teased her huskily.

He felt delicate, slender female hands wrap around his waist and grab his ass. He swallowed. The angle she pulled him into her had his shaft pressed intimately against the fleshy globes of her ass. He felt himself harden in desire.

He wanted her so badly he could barely breathe. For a moment he felt heat sear through him, so strong his knees wobbled. He had never had this level of desire, this ache inside him to possess her forever.

His shaft ached it was so tight and heavy. His balls were drawn tight up against his flesh. He knew he would explode if he didn't sink himself inside her soon.

Gently, he turned Kyli around so she faced him, her belly pressed against his abdomen. She smiled as she closed her eyes against the spray of water. When he pressed her back up against the cold tiles, she wrapped her arms around his ass and drew him in closer to her.

"Something on your mind, Cowboy?" she teased him. He felt his grip on his control slip slightly. He *loved* it when she called him that. It brought back all the sexy memories, both from their past and their time back in the pub.

"Something," he agreed huskily, unable to articulate the desperate desire rushing through him. His shaft swelled so thick he was certain he would burst any second now.

He gently fused their bodies together, ran his cock up and down her damp slit. He knew it was a mixture of her cream and the water from the nozzle. When she arched into him, pressing herself further against the cold tile, bending to try and lodge the tip of him into her, he knew he had her in the palm of his hand.

"Now, now, there's no rush, baby," he chided while the grin spread across his face.

"I want you," she panted, spiking his lust even further. "I want to feel you deep inside me again. It feels like forever since we were together."

Her words, the emotion and feeling behind them, hit him hard in the chest and somehow simultaneously deep in his gut.

This wasn't a game to her, he realized. It had *never* been a game to him, but suddenly with her confession it seemed much more serious.

"It does seem like forever, but then that's not new. It always has been this way between us," he agreed. He moved his hand down to caress her swollen clit, to rub the rough tip of his thumb over the swollen nub. She cried out and he pressed his lips over hers, wanting to drink in the sound of her enjoyment. Wanting to drink *her* inside him.

He drowned in her taste, in the rich warmth from the inside of her mouth. So lost had he become in her and the feminine mysteries of her tongue and taste, he felt a spurt of surprise as she lifted herself up and lodged the tip of his cock inside her creamy pussy.

"Baby," he moaned, wanting to make this time last.

"No," she denied huskily, pushing herself down another inch onto him. "I want this now. I want you deep inside me."

He couldn't help the cry of pleasure that erupted from him as his pleasure spiked even further at her claim. Holding her hips steady, he grunted as the water trickled into his eyes, pounded down onto his head.

"Then take all of me," he claimed. He knew he sounded arrogant, but truly, how could he help it? His woman wanted him desperately enough to force him inside her warmth.

She wanted him badly enough he couldn't help his ego or arrogance from coming out.

He pressed deeply inside her with no more preliminaries, no stroking or coaxing. Just raw, hard, pure him. They both moaned and he could hear the pleasure, the gut-deep desire they both felt.

He wondered if he could die from such sweet satisfaction. The gloving, clasping warmth that his Kyli gave him felt so sweet, so unbearably perfect it was hard to believe.

"Oh, goddess, you feel so good Max!" she moaned in his ear.

Incredibly he swelled even more at her encouragement. "Of course I do," he said, panting at the exertion of trying to speak and not simply pump into her until they both climaxed. "I'm magnificent, remember?"

Slowly, enjoying and drawing out the moment, he withdrew his shaft from the snugness of her sheath.

"Maaaaax," she moaned, he couldn't believe how much he *loved* hearing his name on her lips.

"Yeah, baby?" he teased, licking a path down her throat, tasting the saltiness of her skin and the warmth of the water trickling down her body.

"Max," she begged and pleaded.

Her nails dug into his ass and he loved the pricking sensation, the tiny bite of pain with his pleasure. "You need something, baby?" he queried, nibbling on her neck, loving to draw the moment out. His hips jerked reflexively as he felt her warm, wet index finger circle the rim of his ass.

"Kyli," he warned, indescribably torn between dark, utterly alien desire and confusion.

She lodged the tiniest tip of her finger inside him and the electric sensations, the millions of nerves he didn't even know existed in that dark, virgin place exploded.

Dimly, he heard himself bellow. Utterly against his own volition, his hips thrust forward, pushing them both, crushing them into the wall. He pumped inside her, as deeply as he could possibly reach. The sensation in his ass seemed to link directly with the heat and desire in his balls and cock.

He had never felt anything so erotic, yet so alien at the same time. Never thought to explore his *own* ass, so focused had he been on conquering Kyli's. The pleasure zinging through his system, however, made him wonder what other pleasures they could explore together later.

Unable to hold onto either his control or patience any longer, he drove into Kyli. In and out he moved, almost as if he were possessed. He needed to be inside her, needed to fulfill the pleasure her tiny amount of finger made burn inside him.

"We're going to explore this more later," he promised darkly.

"Absolutely," she panted, arching up into him, almost trying to climb inside his skin. "I look forward to it."

She gasped, and he crushed his lips back onto hers, desperate to enjoy every sound and every taste she could give him. He could feel his balls rise, feel the detonating explosion grow to the brink of pain inside him.

"Come for me," he gasped, unsure whether he insisted or pleaded with her.

"Not a problem," she replied, eyes squeezed tight against the spray of water, or maybe in that same agony of pleasurable pain that he resided in.

And then he could feel her pussy squeeze like a clamp around him. The viselike contractions sent him over the top at the same time as she screamed from the pleasure.

He pumped into her, feeling a purely masculine sense of satisfaction as his seed shot deep inside her, bathing her womb in his essence.

For one spectacular instant, he wished she hadn't taken her suppression shots. In a short, intense series of flashes he could see it all. Kyli in his lodging, rounded with his babe, sated and watching him as she lay on his bed.

He wanted that. Wanted the whole scenario so badly he could taste it. But would she Bond with him? Instead of trying to think himself through that thought, for once in his life, he just blurted it out.

"Marry me," he asked, panting for breath and coming back down from his high. He could feel his knees shake ever so slightly. Incredulous, he realized he had asked the woman he loved to marry him in the bathing unit.

He cleared his throat and stood straighter, shielding her from the now lukewarm spray.

Clearing his throat again, he cast about for words.

"Okay, so it wasn't the most coherent proposal, but maybe give it some thought?"

Unbelievably, he felt his face flush. He couldn't possibly be blushing. He never blushed. Never, ever, *ever* blushed.

"Goddess, it's nothing to *blush* over Max," Kyli said, wonder and stars shining in her eyes.

Max thought she easily was the most beautiful thing he had ever seen.

Hardly believing what he had just done, he stepped back and left the cubicle. He opened the door to the drying chamber and switched the heat up to high. A large part of him simply wished for the planet to explode, or open up and swallow him whole.

*What a dork! Could you fuck that up any more? Proposing in the bathing unit, after some of the best sex ever. You dickhead!*

Feeling dry enough to brave the bathroom, he exited the stall, slightly relieved to find Kyli still in the shower. He headed back into the bedroom and scouted about for some clean boxers.

As he pulled the black plima-silk blend up to sit snugly at his hips he felt his watch silently vibrate. Switching the comm on, he saw a message from Gregor come up on the screen.

Obviously his friend didn't want Kyli to be made aware of the message.

*Remingtons are Tredla's nephews. Their mother is his sister. Go visit Remington at 2300 your time. All has been arranged. Bring Kyli for a witness. Trust me.*

Frowning, a few different scenarios passed through his mind. Any of them could be possible, knowing Gregor and the myriad contacts he had in every position.

Yet a few facts stood out.

The most important one of all was Gregor asking him to trust his word. Max knew beyond a shadow of a doubt Gregor wouldn't lead them both into any harm, particularly not Kyli. Max trusted Gregor, and for his buddy to wring such a promise out of him, it must be imperative both he and Kyli be in the jail cell at 2300 hours.

Looking at his watch, realizing they needed to get ready to leave if they were to be there on time, Max calmly began to dress again. He knew he and Kyli were heading back to the cell where Remington was being held. Not only because Max fully trusted Gregor, but he knew his friend would never ask for something like this unless it were critically important.

That and Gregor would never *insist* Kyli be brought along as a "witness" unless it were serious. Besides, if nothing else, it was always interesting seeing the fruits of Gregor's labors coming into their own.

He heard the door click open, and knew Kyli stood there, watching him. "We need to head back to the jail. Do you have comm details for Roald? Can you ask him to meet us there?"

He could practically feel her frown behind his back.

"Sure. What's up?"

"Not sure yet, we just need to go see Remington now."

He couldn't help but look up as she crossed into his vision. She pulled on the lacy scraps she considered underwear. He felt his mouth water, and bit the inside of his mouth. He didn't have time to seduce her all over again now and beg her properly to Bond with him, or at the very least marry him.

He pulled on his own shirt and pants, socks and shoes, yet he couldn't help himself. He watched Kyli dress herself the whole time out of the corner of his eye. It was as if she were a magnet for him, he simply *had* to watch her lithe body, the way she so casually and easily slipped into her clothes.

When she picked up her small bag and slung it over her shoulder he frowned.

"You shouldn't need that," he started, but she waved a hand dismissingly at him.

"It's my bag and I'm not leaving it here. Besides, I thought we had to go now?"

Shrugging, he gave up. *Who the hell could ever understand women?* He mused to himself.

Opening the door, he waved her through first. Locking it carefully, he kept pace beside Kyli and they headed back towards where Remington was being held.

# Chapter Fifteen
*Gregor's residence*

Gregor set up his comm units in a small semi-circle around himself. One after the other, he sent messages flying out over time and space. His eyes glowed brightly, loving the challenge before him.

His mind had worked at a lightning pace, despite the goddess-awful hour of the morning it was. The Remington half-brothers were Tredla's nephews. That simple fact meant no matter how hard Gregor tried to suppress the information, undoubtedly *someone* would inform the man who Max and Kyli were, and their unusual interest in Am'ah.

Gregor knew it didn't matter what he did now, as they hadn't taken the necessary pains to hide their steps, somehow he would know. And that would put both Max and Kyli in danger. The mission now was to make it patently obvious to all and sundry that Max and Kyli had *nothing* to do with Am'ah's death.

For that, Gregor needed to pull a heap of strings, *fast*.

As he temporarily closed his last message down, he opened up his PCC, squinting at the pale holoscreen in the still-mostly-darkened bedroom. He typed up his plan to date into the flow chart.

Max, Kyli and the current Man-In-Charge of the Jail cell would enter the building at 2300. Three guards utterly loyal to Tredla would be posted out front, and report — eventually — to Tredla their entrance into the jail cell.

At 2305 the assassin would enter, killing two of the guards and then all the prisoners in the jail cell.

Two stories would be circulated. For the general public, an angry old regime supporter is murdered in the jail, proving that the rebels can't control the law and order. The underworld, however, would know that one of the many contracts out on Am'ah's head finally paid out. Tredla would have a decent description of the assassin, who had been paid enough to try and lay low.

Gregor shrugged. Chances were the assassin would be found and murdered, but he was young and full of himself. He had assured the connection Gregor had contacted through a third party that he would happily take the risk for the obscene amount of credits Gregor had offered.

Gregor had encrypted his tracks and covered himself well enough that the hiring would lead to numerous other sources, and not him. As long as Max and Kyli entered the jail on time, and the guard told Tredla as much, then no suspicion of the murder would fall on them, as the murderer would run in after his friends had been documented entering the jail.

No one in their right minds would enter a cell where a mass genocide was about to erupt. They would still be in danger and watched by Tredla, but not because of the murder of his nephew. That would have to be enough for them all to deal with.

Gregor studied his flow chart once more. All the ends were tied up, everything fitted perfectly. Nothing could go wrong as long as things followed the plan. He sat back and sighed. Things so often didn't go to plan, but this once, he had faith, a faith he hadn't had in years.

He cared deeply about his two friends, wanted to see them safe and happy. On such incredibly short notice, it had been the best he could do.

He set up one last holocall, spoke quickly and concisely to the bedraggled man on the other end, outlining the major points of the plan he had set up. When he reached the part where he needed his friend's help, he was interrupted.

*"You want me to organize that? For Remington? Do you think I have a death wish?"* the other man stated incredulously.

"I'll cancel all the tags you owe me," Gregor stated calmly, knowing his buddy, Stott, would go for it for the challenge of the logistics alone. Cancelling any and all debts of honour between them was merely a sweetener. Stott owed Gregor his life from more than one occasion.

Stott groaned and rubbed a weary hand over his face, then agitatedly raked his fingers through his impossibly bright red hair.

*"You're trying to kill me, aren't you? I have a gorgeous woman in my bed, something far more important than I bet you currently have, and you want me to set up an immediate suicide mission?"* Gregor waited a moment, still and patient.

*"Fine,"* he groused, *"send me the –"*

"It should already be downloading on your console." Gregor said, trying hard not to sound smug as he felt. He had known he could count on his buddy. Gregor resisted the strong urge to smile as his friend grunted and severed the connection without another word. He trusted Stott almost as much as he trusted Max and Kyli. He knew every last detail would be set up to perfection and he had done absolutely everything in his power to pull his plan off. The last of his details covered Gregor shut down his PCC and all his comm units except for the one Max would undoubtedly use to call him and probably yell for at least a few minutes once he realized exactly what Gregor had set up.

Setting his alarm, he crawled back into bed and tried to get some rest.

* * * * *

*Back at Randor*

Kyli walked idly through the familiar streets. Her mind ticked away at a steady rate. Her bag gently bounced from her back, a constant reminder of the semi-formed plan she had made back when they had decided to go to Randor.

Kyli gnawed her lower lip in deep thought.

She must have known as soon as Max had entered the dingy pub that she loved him. She had never really stopped, not through all these years. Yet seeing him again, having him and Gregor give her one of her favorite fantasies and then make such sweet and heated love with Max every chance since, had really cemented the fact to her.

She loved him. She wanted to spend the rest of their lives together. She wanted to Bond with him.

Kyli knew how easy it was to marry someone. There were hundreds of reasons people married — business reasons, money reasons, family reasons. All were legal and legitimate, and oh-so-very-easy to dissolve.

Basically marriage was now a contract. And once the terms of said contract were fulfilled, if both parties wished, the marriage was dissolved with little fanfare or issue.

Yet Bonding was a totally different matter. Bonding was permanent. Bonding, if one went to the right priestess, fused your souls together, as well as your hearts and lives.

When Kyli had commed her old friend She'sa, informing her she might be by soon to use her mother's wedding dress and her grandmother's veil—so *very* out of fashion nowadays—she hadn't really formed a plan. Flirting around the outside edges of her mind had been the plan to ask Max for a temporary marriage contract. A trial run so to speak, with the hopes of leading up to a Bonding ceremony.

Yet in the shower he had proposed. *Okay*, she chided to herself, *an awkward and lust-riddled proposal it might have been, but a proposal nevertheless.*

Kyli felt the weight of tradition that surrounded her mother's dress and the expectations that came with it. Her parents had been Bonded nearly thirty years. Her grandparents had been bonded nearly sixty-five years. Scattered though they were, she had been raised in a loving environment and knew the true joy a happy Bonding could bring.

Kyli felt certain she and Max could share that.

In the bathroom, after Max had left, she had again commed her friend.

She'sa had fought right beside her the entire time she had been working with the Rebels. Wild, brave, fierce She'sa. She was a full-fledged priestess of Randor. Her friend truly believed deep in her soul in the strength and power of the warrior women the planet worshiped. And now she also stood second in line to the rulership of Randor. Llelo was her elder and incredibly protective, brother.

When Max had mentioned coming back here, Kyli knew their union—whatever union they might chose—would be truly blessed if She'sa joined them. Between her friend joining them, and her mother's blue dress—blue for the longevity of the sky, silver piping for the excitement of the stars—Kyli knew she and Max could have it all.

She had messaged She'sa, not certain if her friend was in meditation or not. She felt her wrist vibrate with what she hoped to be an answering message.

*Sounds interesting, my friend. This feels incredibly right. I'm in. Comm me details when you know. S.*

Kyli smiled. Now, how to drop the bomb to Max? Randor had no waiting period, no blood tests, almost no paperwork. All you needed was a priestess willing to join you. And She'sa certainly fit the bill.

She ran into the back of Max. He had stopped and she had been so lost in her own musings, she had failed to notice.

"Oof. What gives, Max?"

"The guard has changed," he said softly. Kyli stepped around him and noticed the guard by the front door was indeed a different one than a few hours previous when they had entered.

Striding ahead of her, Max took out his Force identification. Kyli followed a pace behind. She listened to Max introduce himself and watched the guard closely. She had the feeling that something was strange...almost out of place. She couldn't tell what it was, other than instinct. But something seemed very off with the whole situation.

The guard took the proffered identification and studied it closely. This also made her feel uneasy. She knew the ID checked out, but why would a normal guard pay so close attention to something as common as the identification?

Worse, after handing Max his case back, the guard only gave her ID the briefest of flickering glances. She felt unbelieving how he obviously cast her aside as any semblance of a threat.

The guard shrugged and stepped aside to let them both enter. Before they had even left the guard's hearing range and she could comment to Max, they heard the dim echoes of Roald yelling. The ravings only became more profane and louder as they entered into the main room.

"I don't give a flying frugrum who you think commed the orders in, I do *not* want Jackson and Peters guarding these doors! What the hell kind of fool do you think I am?"

Kyli halted outside the small office door with Max, unsure whether to enter or not. It looked obvious that something was up, she just couldn't really tell what.

"Yes, I bloody well know they've not been formally charged yet, but with one Remington captive here and the other floating around goddess knows where do you really think I want my two *least* trustworthy—"

Kyli felt amazed. Much like in any combat situation the scene changed from rather amusing, to utter chaos in the space of a heartbeat.

The unmistakable sound of a bottle bomb going off just inside the foyer of the building blasted through the long corridor, shattering many of the windows and creating a white noise. Dimly, as if from a great distance or through a badly tuned set of headphones, Kyli could hear people shouting, and what sounded like keys rattling, which she soon knew was actually laser fire.

Just as these thoughts clicked through her mind, she automatically reached for her beamer, only to be tackled to the ground. Struggling, trying to free her legs to get a solid kick in, only the distinctive scent of Max halted her. Twisting, she looked into his dark face, his mouth set firmly downward.

"Quit struggling, woman. Don't get messed up in this," he insisted.

"But—" she tried to argue, but just got a steady palm held across her mouth for her troubles.

"Forget it Kyli, I'm calling the shots."

Kyli frowned, gathered her wits. *She* had all the experience on this planet, *she* knew the layout best. *How dare he*—? Even her thoughts were cut off as another explosion rocked the building.

Raising her arms to cover her head, Kyli instinctively curled into the fetal position, trying to protect her body from the broken glass and mortar flying everywhere. There were a few more bursts of laser fire and everything fell eerily silent.

Kyli shuffled, wanting to get out from underneath Max and see what had happened.

"Well I'll be damned," she heard Roald clearly shout, obviously still somewhat deaf from the explosions.

As soon as Max raised his weight from her body she stood up like a shot. Both of them crossed over into the corridor that led to the cells, but they didn't have to move far. Three sprawled bodies lay in the hallway. The prisoners had been shot while escaping.

Blood and mess was scattered everywhere. Kyli was a seasoned merc, but she still felt her legs wobble ever so slightly. It was a rare occurrence for her or anyone to actually see these bloody remains of combat. Usually she and her group were inside, or even heading back home, while others cleaned up the mess.

She felt Max's arm come across her shoulder and turn her away.

"Grab your bag and meet me out the front, baby. See how much damage was done to people passing by."

Grateful for once to have something meaningful to do, Kyli raced out the front. She didn't spill her guts, but as she gulped in deep lungful of the fresh air, she felt her head steady and her heartbeat slow down.

After a moment, she slung her bag from her listless hand onto her back and checked over the front of the building. The guard who had been there earlier had either headed inside and she hadn't noticed him or he had deserted. The bottle bombs had created a small amount of wreckage along the front surface of the building but nothing major.

Bottle bombs were small, kiddie bombs. Anyone could make them and while they made a lot of noise and smoke, they did little damage unless one stood too close to them when they exploded.

Frowning, Kyli realized that while people now milled around in curiosity, no one screamed out, no one wailed. In fact, there were no casualties and seemingly no victims at all. Windows were smashed and a small smoking hole resided near the explosion point, but that was all.

Feeling much more under control, Kyli headed back inside. Catching up with Max, she looked at him and shrugged her shoulders.

"Dunno where the guard is, but other than some structural damage and the windows, nothing's wrong. No people got hurt at all. Obviously we got lucky."

"More than lucky," he agreed solemnly. He turned to Roald who scratched his head, a symbol she recognized of him not understanding and thinking.

"Damndest thing, Kyli. Some mongrel broke in the back, shot two of my men, released the three prisoners, shot them as they escaped, and then left."

Kyli blinked, remembering Roald's shouted conversation about his distrust of the guards who had been assigned. Two of whom were dead, the other missing. And Remington mysteriously shot along with two other captives.

It felt so neat she knew Gregor had to have something to do with it. "Um," she started to say, "so what do we do now?"

Roald smiled slightly, lifting out his comm unit. "Now, my dear, we comm the Army and start the clean up. Nothing we could have done. Hang on a second and I'll grab your long-term comm details and then you'd better move on out. Reporters will be here any second, and you know what they're like."

Max grinned and slung an arm around her. Kyli shook her head and started typing out their details and messaging it through to Roald's comm unit.

"Like you said, nothing any of us could do. Bloody shame, isn't it?"

Roald nodded and waved them away as he started to speak to his superior. Much swearing ensued as reporters started literally climbing in through the holes in the back wall. Various guards, brought in by the noises of the explosions, hastened to gather the corpses and hide them from view.

"Goddess damn it!" Roald shouted as a particularly skinny young woman began to shove a comm in his face and babble for a quote. "You pack of bloody vultures, get the hell out of here or I'll slap the lot of you with restraining orders for so damn long your children's children won't be able to get on the Reporters League!"

Max and Kyli didn't even glance at each other, they simply turned and left while holo-cameras whirled and people began to shout questions at them.

Kyli let Max take her arm and led her outside into the sunshine. They started at a jog, and after Kyli took them down a couple of quick successive turns, they stopped, knowing they had lost anyone who might have followed. Most of the story was with Roald anyway, so Kyli felt no guilt.

Kyli got her bearings, then decided it was time she and Max really got down to business. She took his arm, checked to see that nothing had fallen from her bag, and took a quick left.

Time to go to the Temple.

# Chapter Sixteen

"So where are we heading?" Max asked for the zillionth time.

Kyli smiled, enjoying how curious he was, and how he couldn't stop trying to get her to explain where she led them. *Let him wonder*, she decided.

"I told you. I just want to pop in on a friend of mine before we head back. She'd never forgive me for not saying hi while I was here." Tugging his hand more forcefully than needed, Kyli smiled as he cursed.

"Look, we're nearly there. And it's not like you have anything else planned for the next fifteen minutes."

"Actually," he purred, lifting her off her feet and setting her down against a wall, "I had plenty planned."

With that he kissed her fiercely, opening her mouth with his and thrusting his tongue between her lips. She moaned, opening up to the taste of him. She reached out to pull his shoulders down, to bring him as close to her as possible. She forgot her plans, forgot her meeting with She'sa and how she was supposed to be planning her strategy to convince Max to Bond with her.

She forgot everything, including where they were and what the last day and a half had been like. All she knew was Max was kissing her and he tasted divine.

"No," she moaned as he pulled away, wanting the kiss to go on for eternity.

"I thought we had a very important person to meet?" he teased. Kyli blinked, her mind coming back into focus. She hit Max, knowing it wouldn't hurt him in the least.

"Beast! If she refuses my favor because you distracted me—!"

"What favor? What could this woman give you that I can't?"

Kyli smiled secretively as she halted outside the temple doors. Nothing outwardly proclaimed it as a sacred site to those who didn't know. Kyli knew the carvings on either side of the door were wards of protection and fertility. She knew the animal faces represented the Spiritual Guardians and most importantly of all, she knew the astrological symbols on each other four points of the door were not only for lifelong luck, but also as a special blessing to couples who entered.

It was easily the most holy place she had ever entered, and been allowed to stay within. From the uneasy way Max looked about him, she knew he could feel the sacredness of the spot as well.

*Excellent.* "Why Max, my friend is the High Priestess of the Order here. I thought we could Bond before we went home."

She grinned, knowing this would knock the wind from his sails. She knew in the future it would be so hard to stay one step ahead of him. It already took all her effort to stay that way. So she wanted this to be big.

As she had hoped, Max just gaped at her.

"Here?" he queried. She smiled up at him, pleased he sensed how important this place was, both to her and to anyone who entered.

"Here," she said firmly, knocking on the door and not being surprised when it seemingly opened itself. Reaching back, she grabbed Max's hand.

"Come on. I'll introduce you to She'sa."

She led her lover into the main foyer, a large, cool place that seemed almost sentient. A small pool trickled in one corner, vegetation sprung up from hidden crevices. A number of opened doorways were scattered around the room.

Kyli led them over to one of many recliners in semi-hidden alcoves. Nothing was truly hidden from She'sa or any of the other priestesses in this temple. Yet Kyli knew from previous experience one could never go where one wasn't wanted. The temple somehow just made the path you took double back on itself.

It was the perfect place for meditation and privacy. If you only needed to see one person, then only that person would notice you. It always felt simultaneously uncanny and really cool to Kyli. The main reason she knew such privacy existed was because doorways that she *knew* on one day would lead to a certain room, the next day or even the next hour led to a completely different place.

That was why she had told She'sa she would *always* await her in the foyer. No sense in wandering around completely lost—unless that happened to be her reason for entering the temple.

The temple's almost innate sense of the wishes and desires of its occupants was but one reason she loved this place more than any other.

"Sit down with me and let me explain." Kyli said, gesturing Max to a couch in a small alcove near the pool.

She casually dropped her bag on the floor near the seat, knowing it was completely safe.

"She'sa and I met during the Rebels fight. I didn't know it for a while, but she's Llelo's sister, now the second in line to rule. We became very good friends. I spent my last night here, just before I came home. We talked through many a night and on our last one she made me promise if I ever met a man I wanted to Bond with, I'd bring him to her and she'd bless our union. She's very powerful, easily the most powerful priestess I've ever met. I had been thinking about this since our first night together. You said you wanted to marry, so I'm asking if we can Bond instead."

"Asking?" Max teased, running his finger along the bottom of her lip. Kyli resisted the impulse to lick his finger, to suck it in her mouth. "I thought a person asking to Bond had to be down on one knee, begging."

Kyli smiled. "You can make me beg all you like when we get back home."

Max leaned forward, running his lips softly against hers.

"I like the sound of that. You promise?"

"A Bond-promise," she said softly, knowing he was agreeing despite his teasing.

"Well then, I better have a Bond-mate to keep that promise."

Kyli turned her head up to accept the kiss, the promise they were sharing between them. She knew everything had happened so fast, but she couldn't help it. Without realizing it she had been waiting for this man for years, been searching for someone even half as sexy and dominant. She had never forgotten or healed fully from him.

Now, together, they could forge their own path.

She heard someone clear their throat behind where they sat. Smiling, she reached out to hold Max's hand. She knew he would be defensive because neither of them had heard her approach. But that was just She'sa.

"I see you wasted no time, Kyli."

Kyli grinned, standing up to hug her friend warmly.

"Actually She, Max is the one who nabbed me. Even stole my thunder and asked me to Bond with him this morning." Reluctantly letting her friend go, she reached out to take her hand.

"As soon as I knew we were coming here I figured I'd propose and get you to do the honors of Bonding and blessing us. Besides, you have my dress, I had to bring my special jewelry."

She let go of her friend's hand and opened her bag, taking out a sparkling blue and silver jeweled collar necklace.

"*That's* what you've been carrying around all this time?" Max said, incredulous. "Jewels?"

Kyli frowned and glared at him. "My mother's ancestral jewels. She'sa has my mother's dress," she explained severely. "You should know damn well how important history and ancestry is to any Bonding."

Max grinned sheepishly at both She'sa and her.

"Sorry. I just couldn't believe you had carried that around with us so long. But if your friend is willing…"

She'sa looked over Max carefully. Kyli held her breath. Nothing she could say would alter She'sa's opinion. She would make her own judgment call.

"He makes you happy?" She'sa questioned, not even looking at her.

Kyli turned to Max, to stare in his eyes. Dark eyes that promised untold nights of passion, pleasure and companionship.

"Oh yeah, She, he makes me very happy."

"And you will treat her with love and respect? With desire and openness?" She'sa demanded, still staring hard at Max.

"Yes, ma'am," he concurred. She'sa nodded and for the first time turned to face Kyli, smiling into her eyes and embracing her.

"Come with me, darling. You need to get dressed. Max, please wait here a moment."

Kyli let She'sa lead her through a doorway and into a small room. A full-length holo-mirror filled one wall, small racks and boxes next to it would easily hold her meager belongings.

"Get dressed, you'll find everything there. I'll go back and get your man."

Kyli turned back to face her friend.

"Thank you She'sa."

She'sa smiled and hugged her again.

"It is fine. He is a good man, he will be perfect for you." Kyli grinned when she felt She'sa press a hand against her stomach. An alien warmth shot through her. It didn't feel sexual, but rather like a warm hand passing through her stomach and moving lower. She felt a slight flutter, a shakiness zing through her, and then all returned to normal. "I do believe you will create a child before the next full cycle, my friend. You are almost ripe."

Kyli frowned.

"But I've had my suppression shots."

She'sa smiled in that annoyingly mysterious way she had.

"Make sure you check the times of your shots. Ask your man. He is already fertile as he got a clean bill of health, not another suppression shot. He had been planning to be celibate the next sixmonth. You will be fertile before the next moon, too. You felt the heat in your womb just now, your returning fertility."

Kyli frowned and counted back the months, checking on her personal unit the dates of her last injections. Sure enough, in two weeks time, her suppression shots would run out.

Kyli smiled, knowing tonight would bring interesting conversations with Max.

"Cool. Thanks for the heads up, She."

She watched her friend glide to the door, winking as she shut it behind her.

"What are Priestess friends for?"

As the door *thunked* its closure behind her, Kyli quickly stripped and headed towards the small heated pool in one corner. She wanted to bathe the dust and grime from her body, and knew it would take forever to do up the old-style buttons on the dress. Besides, She'sa would be back soon to start the ceremony.

And then there would be the Bonding night, which set her heart pounding and her mouth watering.

She could hardly wait.

# Chapter Seventeen

Max sat on the couch after Kyli had left him, staring into the slowly trickling pool of water.

*Bonding with Kyli*, he mused.

While he knew he had no doubts, a smart man still thought through the consequences of his actions before jumping in with both feet. Marriage was one thing, a contract that was easily negated once the terms had come to pass. Nowadays a marriage could be based on almost anything, as long as it stated the terms in the contract.

Many people married for children, the creation of or naming after birth. Once said child came into the world the marriage could easily be made void. Any military or government agent could make it so. Some people married for a certain length of time, for companionship or just to see whether they would be suited to Bond.

As long as one had a contract, and to marry one must have one, anything in the terms agreed upon were legal.

Bonding, on the other hand, was completely different. A contract was signed, but there the similarities ended. The Bonding contract had been made centuries ago, and was cast in iron. No pleading, no amount of money or appeals could overturn the terms. The *lifelong* terms.

The pair was joined for life, end of story. Yet the other part of the contract, the more scoffed-at terms, seemed so much more real here in this sacred temple.

It was whispered amongst the men, that if a woman could induce you to Bond with her, then your souls fused, your very essences joined that broken circle.

Many, many years ago, back in school, Max had learned of the theory written by Sophocles—or was it Aristotle?—that men and women were two halves of one circle, broken when the world had been created.

Bonding, it had always been whispered, fused those two halves together. That was why you could only be bonded by a Priest or Priestess. They had to ascertain that the couple were, indeed, the broken halves of the circle. Bonded mates who were not truly destined, more often than not in the past had ended up living in abject misery for all their life.

In his heart, Max knew he and Kyli were the two parts of a circle, knew he loved her. Yet Bonding was such a serious step, such a *permanent* step, he hesitated.

"Wise of you, my boy," came a familiar voice from behind him. Refusing to curse—how the hell did she sneak up on him time and time again?—Max turned to face Kyli's friend.

"She'sa," he stood, "Kyli's okay?"

The Priestess smiled. Her long blonde hair fell to her waist in ripples. Her blue robes somehow concealed her form, yet let any man know a lush, curvaceous body lay underneath.

Having spent ten minutes in the temple, he knew the art of concealing and revealing at the same time was everywhere here.

"Kyli is getting herself prepared for the ceremony. I think it's a good sign you were contemplating it yourself.

You do understand the significance of the ceremony, don't you?"

Max nodded. "Sure, every child is taught how important it is. Fusing the two halves back together, rejoining the souls. No backing out or crying off once the deed is done."

She'sa tilted her head.

"Interesting, such a masculine response. Let's make a light joke of it so I won't have to acknowledge the seriousness of the situation." She watched as Max let a sheepish smile cross his face as the Priestess shook her head in feminine resignation. "Cross the galaxy," she murmured, "and men are all the same. Such is the way."

Max grinned, "Well, my Priestess, we are a simple lot."

He felt amazed as the Priestess snorted. She waved him to follow her and she led him through the same door she had taken Kyli. Max grinned. Maybe they could do this right now and he could get to the private celebrations.

He looked forward to the Bonding celebrations. He and Kyli, a large bed, and a whole evening ahead of them.

Instead, they walked down a long corridor with no doors or windows. At the end of the corridor stood one door, which She'sa opened.

"You'll find everything you need in here. Prepare yourself, as if for a ritual. Bathe yourself and I'll be back for you when you're completed."

Max frowned. He *knew* Kyli should be here, yet she was nowhere to be seen.

"Where's Kyli?" he asked, confused.

"In another chamber, preparing herself. The temple didn't want the two of you to view each other until the ceremony, and so we passed her door and you did not see it."

Max entered the room and looked around.

"You'll be back for me?" he checked, uneasy in a situation where he had no control whatsoever.

She'sa nodded. "As soon as you've prepared yourself. I need to set up the Bonding chamber for you both."

Max shrugged and watched as the Priestess closed the door behind her. He walked over to the wardrobe, not at all surprised to find a suit exactly his size hanging in the space.

Crossing over to the bathing chamber, he picked up the scented bathing lotion and took a whiff. It appeared to be a masculine scent, vaguely reminiscent of the rain drenching a forest. Nodding, he stripped and entered the unit.

Scrubbing, he amused himself with thoughts of what he could do with Kyli tonight. What he could do *to* Kyli tonight, more importantly.

Grinning, he ignored his hardening shaft. He felt certain after the ceremony he would need all his strength. If they were going to Bond, going to spend their whole lives together, they might as well start off on the right foot.

*Sexual marathon* echoed through his head. Max grinned widely. He wondered if that was his thought, the Priestess', or maybe he'd been picking up on Kyli's wishes?

Quickly rinsing, becoming more eager every moment, he dried himself and dressed in the suit provided for him.

Gathering his clothes in the small bag, he was running his hands through his hair, combing the last of the tangles from it, when the door opened again. She'sa walked through, in a similar but vaguely different robe.

"The time is right," she said, mysterious in the way Priests and Priestesses across the galaxy seemed to be.

Smiling, looking forward to the ceremony, Max followed the woman back out into the corridor. He knew he was being led to Kyli, to their Bonding ceremony.

He followed impatiently, hard and ready for his mate.

# Chapter Eighteen

Max stood in what appeared to be a small chamber. Having walked through a number of corridors, all appearing to lead nowhere, he knew what he *thought* he saw wasn't necessarily what was there.

He stood in a pale blue light, the source of which he could not find, and tried not to tap his foot or jiggle in impatience. She'sa had informed him Kyli was on her way, and so he waited.

Even though the suit was exactly his size, *how* it had managed to appear in his closet he didn't want to know. The white pleated shirt scratched at his sensitized skin and in his nerves the jacket began to feel constricting.

Yet when the door had opened to admit the Priestess, she had looked him up and down and then smiled brightly.

"You'll make her catch her breath. You look good," she had said, and so here he stood about to tie himself for all eternity to the woman he loved in a shirt that scratched, a jacket he longed to remove, and pants that with the state of his erection were beginning to feel way too tight.

He had to be in love, otherwise he would have to label himself the biggest fool who ever existed. But once he heard a noise behind him—everyone here seemed to be able to creep up on him—he turned slightly.

Only to catch *his* breath. Kyli looked absolutely stunning.

Her mother's gown fit like a glove. The dark midnight blue material shimmered against her pale skin, setting off her blue eyes and dark locks. The silver thread glimmered in the light, twinkling merrily and reflecting from the silver and blue necklace that sparkled around her throat.

She looked the most beautiful sight he had ever had the pleasure of viewing. Her thin veil did nothing to conceal her huge grin or her gorgeous features. As she slowly walked toward him, he tried to catch his breath and shut his mouth.

After what felt like an eternity, she reached his side and he held out a hand. She smiled widely and took it. He stared deeply into her eyes, which glittered in the blue light. He could see forever there, children, happiness, lots of better-than-fantastic sex, and more, they would be helpmates. Sure, he could see some volatile arguments, but the make-up sex afterwards would cure those issues.

He could see their future, the two of them always together, as easily as if it were a book he could read.

She'sa cleared her throat and grabbed his attention.

She looked from Kyli to him, and then back to her friend again.

"You both know how serious a Bonding it is. This is no contract, easily made and easily completed. This is a merging of your souls. It's a serious step, and one that shouldn't be taken lightly. Really, there is little use for most of the rituals people do to try and help their Bonding be a happy one. You don't need to drink from the same goblet, you don't need to exchange flowers and words of praise. All you really need to do is make sure your commitment is strong and true."

Max felt a frission of shock as She'sa looked directly at him and grinned widely.

"And, of course, have orgasmic sex to actually merge your souls together."

Kyli grinned at her friend and chuckled.

"Well, that *was* always my favorite part of it."

Max felt himself, astoundingly, blush at the two women who watched him as if he were a stud about to perform for them.

She'sa grinned and waved a hand to them. "Take each other's hands."

Max turned to face Kyli. Holding her hands gently, he felt a soft current run between them. An understanding, a connection. Almost as if they already shared a special Bond.

"Kyli," She'sa said softly, "repeat after me. In the eyes of the goddess, I proclaim you to be my chosen Bondmate."

Max felt his heart swell as Kyli clearly uttered the words. He knew she spoke them to him, yet he could easily imagine the goddess present, hearing and nodding indulgently.

"Max, repeat after me. In the eyes of the goddess, I proclaim you to be my chosen Bondmate."

Max easily spoke the words, as they came to his lips of their own volition, as if he had been waiting to say them forever. When he finished the word "Bondmate", he could sense a connection snap between him and Kyli. He felt a solid thread bind his heart to hers.

He was getting lightheaded, almost as if he had drunk too much Blue or Purple Vodka. It seemed like the alcohol was freeing him from his inhibitions and simultaneously clearing his mind.

He barely noticed as She'sa took a few steps backwards, and with a smile in her voice said, "Now you must consummate the bond. Enjoy yourselves, kids."

Still staring deeply into Kyli's eyes, Max slowly took the small step needed to close the distance between them. He lifted the veil, settling it behind her head. Ignoring everything in the small, dimly lit room, he wrapped Kyli in his embrace.

"Hello, Bondmate," he murmured. He loved the way Kyli's eyes shone, the way her smile covered her whole face and lit her up from within.

"Hello, Bondmate," she repeated, lifting her hand to pull his head down to hers.

He kissed her. A gentle, soft, chaste kiss. He simply pressed his lips to hers, happiness welling within him that she was his and no other's. He had to smile when Kyli groaned deep inside her throat and lowered her hands to pull his ass closer to her. He ground his erection against the silky material of her long, flowing gown.

Reluctantly he pulled his mouth away.

"I know we have forever," he started, surprised with how out of breath he sounded, "but I do believe you have far too many clothes on. I really don't want to lose control and rip something."

Kyli smiled and turned her back. Max groaned.

"Is this a form of self-inflicted torture? How many damned buttons do you have?"

Determined to prove himself, Max began to undo the buttons. They were very rare and exceedingly Old World. Tiny little contraptions designed then and now to drive a man insane with lust. He couldn't help muttering under his breath as he slowly, painstakingly undid the small things.

He saw Kyli's shoulders shake with laughter.

"You did this just to tease me, didn't you?" he grumbled.

"No, love," she insisted, laughter nearly choking her. "But I must admit, seeing a grown warrior like yourself cursing two dozen tiny pearl buttons does make one laugh."

Finally, after what felt like forever, he had undone all the buttons. The Old World dress, elegant and traditional in its simplicity gaped to the very bottom of her back, and he easily helped her step out of it. He admired her firm body, delicately encased in ivory lace, a matching bra and panties set, and thigh high stockings with garters and high-heeled shoes.

For some reason, both their sets of clothing seemed to be completely Old World. It bespoke tradition and familiarity. Just as for many, many millennia in the past this style of clothing had joined men and women together, so too did they follow in their footsteps.

Max turned Kyli around in his arms.

"Shall we keep the jewels on? They look divine with your eyes and the light."

Kyli simply nodded, her eyes full of love and emotion. The sparkle in her eyes seemed even brighter than the sparkle at her throat.

"Wow," he proclaimed, "I will never again tease you for carting that bag around with us the whole time. This ivory underwear set is spectacular, must have cost you a fortune to get commissioned. And the necklace...it takes my breath away. "

Kyli smiled and wrapped her arms around his neck.

"A girl's gotta be prepared," she insisted.

Max bent down and fiercely took her mouth with his. Thrusting his tongue inside her mouth, he tasted her. She moaned and arched into him, and that only added to his hunger for her. She tasted warm, faintly of mint and spice. She was all Kyli and completely his.

He felt his erection strain even further, desperately wanting to claim what belonged to him.

Almost together, they decided they couldn't wait any longer. Hands scrabbled to remove his jacket and to tear his shirt from his chest. To loosen his pants.

They giggled like children when his shoes became caught in his pants. Max looked briefly around, amazed at how dark most of the room was. The blue light still shone, yet he couldn't even see the walls, so dark was the shadows.

Thankfully, he saw a small double bed just on the edge of the light source. He nodded at it, indicating to Kyli where they should move. Trying not to ruin his clothes, which weren't even his, he shuffled over to the bed and sat on its edge.

"Poor baby," Kyli soothed him in a cooing voice. "Are we a bit tangled up?"

Growling incoherently, Max began to tug his shoes from his feet. Letting them both fall to the floor, he stood unsteadily, lust having driven his blood south, and shed his pants and socks in rapid order.

Feeling like the most powerful being in the galaxy, he lifted Kyli into his arms and threw her gently on the bed.

She bounced once and he followed her down, caging her in his arms.

"Now *you're* the one overdressed, my dear. I just have my boxers on, while you still have all that magnificent get-up on."

He loved hearing her husky laugh, loved the way it lit up her eyes and made her face sparkle in happiness. Reverently, wanting to show her how special she felt to him, he removed her heels. Tossing them away from the bed, they both smiled at each other at the *thunk* that sounded as each one struck the floor.

Slowly, letting his fingers trail over the pockets of skin her stockings exposed, he unsnapped the thigh highs from her garters. When all four snaps were free, he unrolled the shimmering silk.

He took his time as he carefully removed the silk, exposing her skin. He loved watching the flush of sexual awareness creep over her breasts and chest. He enjoyed watching her squirm, knowing full well the sensations his gentle caress with barely his fingertips evoked in her. His hands might be rough, might have fought more days than they lay idle. Yet he loved being able to touch her gently, caress her satin-soft skin and bring this reaction from her.

The seconds ticked by, becoming minutes. Finally he removed one stocking from her foot. Carelessly, he dropped the delicate piece of silk on the covers and bent to pay homage to the leg he had unwrapped. Smooth, sleek muscles lay under the soft skin of her leg, her unpolished toenails making him smile. Kyli might not be the most feminine woman he knew, but she sure as hell was the hottest.

He gently massaged the foot he held, rubbing the ball of the foot and working his way up to the toes. He enjoyed the view of Kyli wriggling, loved finding her ticklish spots.

And then he began with the second stocking.

He didn't really understand where his patience sprang from. He was hot and hard, he had just Bonded with the woman of his dreams, and yet he wanted to make this special, wanted her to never forget these moments. But more, he wanted to show her he cherished her. Wanted her to know she was special and held a place in his heart.

He wanted to show her he could be just as careful and gentle with her as any other man. The fact he could also be the dominant, aggressive man of her fantasies just made them that much more suited.

At long last he removed the second stocking, and he had to smile as a strangled sound came from Kyli. She sat up suddenly, pushing him off balance. She shoved him down onto the bed and straddled him.

"I know you're being wonderful, but right now I need you more than I need my next breath," she panted, twisting her arms behind her to unclasp her bra. "I love that you're showing me you can be gentle and tender. And trust me, I love it. But right now, I need to ride you."

Max laughed.

"What happened to romance? What happened to this being the most special night of our lives?" he teased, catching his breath as her lacy panties ripped in her haste to remove them.

"Next time," she promised, making her voice deeper to sound just like him, "we'll do tender and slow next time. Right now," she began to pull his boxers from him. He lifted his hips, helpless to stop her and secretly not even wanting to. "Right now, I need you to be inside me or I just might die."

Without any further warning, Kyli pressed herself down over him, sheathing his throbbing cock deep inside her pussy. They both moaned. Max couldn't swear how it felt for Kyli, but he felt like he filled her so tightly, if she had been any smaller or he any thicker, they would have both burst.

If his eyes hadn't been closed, if he hadn't been half out of his mind with lust, Max might never have heard the smaller, softer gasp from behind them. His eyes sprang open as he bent his head backwards, searching.

*She'sa had never left the room,* he suddenly realized.

Quick as a blink, he grabbed Kyli's shoulders and reversed their position on the bed. His body now covered her nakedness from anyone who might be watching.

"What?" Kyli squeaked. "I thought I was taking control."

"Is She'sa still here?" he queried, having unimaginable problems trying to regain his control.

Kyli snickered, "Well, of course she is. She has to make sure we consummate the Bonding, she has to know our souls merge. She can't do that from another room, can she?"

Max stared, unbelieving. "You don't mind she's watching?"

Kyli smiled and brought his face closer to hers, "Not this once, no. But at the moment there's nothing to watch, is there?"

Max relaxed. "Well then, let's give her an eyeful."

Moving his hands down to cradle her hips, he lifted her slightly for a better angle of penetration. He thrust deeply inside her, moving her hips until he felt himself rubbing against her G-spot. As the friction caused Kyli to arch and clench her inner muscles, all thoughts of the Priestess watching them disappeared.

He could only focus on Kyli.

# Chapter Nineteen

Kyli moaned, her back arched so much she felt certain she'd have to work out at the gym the following morning just to get the kinks out and relax her muscles. Being truthful, she did feel a bit odd with the knowledge She'sa watched them. Yet at the same time it turned her on more.

Kyli had never felt this fluttery excitement at showing her lover off to someone else. She'sa was a good friend, a loyal friend. As a Priestess she would never break her vows and gossip about their sex, or what occurred during this ceremony.

The old adage "What occurs at a Bonding, remains at a Bonding" was a sacred vow, a knowing. Kyli felt her head roll back onto the soft mattress. She could feel the pressure inside her, the need to climax rush through her.

The sexual tension between them grew. She teased Max by tightening her internal muscles, clamping even tighter around his shaft. In return, he thrust deeply, moving her like a dance partner so his thick shaft rubbed past her G-spot. The longer they prolonged the inevitable climax, the more they teased each other in the intimate give and take of making love, Kyli could feel the strangest phenomenon begin to take shape.

As her body grew tenser, the excitement rising more and more, she could feel a huge wave of emotion grow inside her. Yet simultaneously, she felt brief flashes of a purely masculine satisfaction.

It took her a moment to realize what, exactly, she could feel during these images, so alien was the emotion. Yet in a flash of intuition, she clicked to the fact the dark, intense sensations flowing through her mind were masculine, and thus unknown to her.

They were a deep, intense satisfaction. A masculine possessiveness. If she had to verbalize the emotions, they would be something akin to a man's boasting to another "She's mine," or maybe "She's a magnificent fuck." They were raw, earthy, primitive feeling.

And in another image of rare feminine insight, she recognized the emotions must be what Max felt at the moment. The obvious conclusion would be he could feel the clawing need and satisfaction she, too could feel.

"Do you feel it?" she asked him, startled at just how little breath she had.

"Baby," he panted, thrusting even harder, "I'm certainly feeling something."

"No," she laughed, losing more of her breath, "I meant can you feel that...knowing between us?"

She watched Max's brow crease in thought. "Yeah, not surprisingly you want to come, but you also know as if you're about to explode for the immense pleasure."

Kyli smiled wryly at the intense look of smug, utterly masculine satisfaction crossing his features.

"You think I'm a good fuck."

Kyli rolled her eyes. *So much for romance!*

Before she could question him any further, Max licked his thumb, his eyes capturing hers as he did it. Somehow that one act seemed even more erotic, more sensual, than all the touching and playing they had done previously.

Her eyes remained glued to his. There lay a wealth of possession, of satisfaction and ownership inside those eyes. Sure, she was a modern merc, independent and determined to follow the beat of her own way, yet a smaller, more intimate part of her knew she would remain with Max forever. Would happily do anything to follow and help him, remain with him all their days.

And then his wet thumb caressed her clit.

She flew apart, every thought scattered to the winds.

She moaned, deep and low inside her throat.

"Goddess," Max breathed, still stroking her clit, "I can feel your orgasm rip through you. It's…different from how a man feels it."

Static filled her ears, Kyli couldn't be certain if he said more or not. Squeezing her eyes shut she could only feel the ripples of the climax flow over her skin and muscles. The tiny, familiar jolts of pleasure sang through her system as she came down from her high.

Max continued to stroke her clit, engorged and sensitive as it was. His touch had become lighter, but it still created a fire inside her. Determined to not be passive any longer, Kyli reached underneath them and tried to stroke his balls.

"Here," Max chuckled, "let's try to be creative."

Quickly, not letting her give any input, he lifted both her legs and, spreading them wide apart, placed one over each shoulder.

"Max," she moaned, unable to think clearly again. The action of raising her legs had contracted her passage, giving him a tighter sheath, squeezing his cock. The raised position of her legs let him thrust even deeper. His long cock already had a mighty level of penetration.

After her first climax she had opened up more, embraced him more. This deeper penetration had him in her to the hilt. She felt stuffed full and rejoiced in the extra level of deepness.

Holding one of her legs steady with one hand, Max grasped her hip with the other and drew her closer.

"Perfect," she purred, now able to fondle his balls. When he grunted, she knew they wouldn't last much longer. She could simultaneously feel the regrowing urgency inside herself, as well as the pressure building inside Max.

She concentrated on him, on the feelings she received from him. He felt immense pleasure in her soft, gentle caressing of his balls, but a muted frustration as well. He wanted to thrust inside her until he exploded. He didn't want to hold back.

Kyli smiled. She couldn't reach Max's face to draw him down and kiss him from this position, but she could certainly tease and taunt him.

"Max," she purred, stroking his balls and rolling them gently in both of her hands. "I want you to fuck me hard. I want you to plunge so deeply inside me you'll never get out." She felt his breath coming faster, harder. She gloried in the feminine power she held. "I want you to merge your soul with mine so we will never be free of each other. I want to feel you come, both your seed hot and deep inside my body, but also that intense satisfaction of losing your head and letting go of your control as you climax."

As she spoke her words, having no idea where they came from, Kyli could feel Max's cock stiffen inside her. She could feel the rumbling beginning of his climax, and knew they were about to be joined forever. She threw her arms free, splaying her body and somehow feeling her mind and soul open to him.

She trusted Max, would follow him anywhere, do anything for him. She knew with a soul-deep certainty they would grow old and live happily together.

She opened her mind and heart to him.

As Max bellowed, she felt the first deep thrust and spurt of his cock, bathing her womb with his seed. He let go of her legs and they fell to each side, twining around his hips to draw him even deeper inside her. She couldn't help herself. She grabbed him and brought him close, so his head buried in her neck.

"Oh Kyli, goddess you feel good," he said and she felt his chest seemingly melt to merge inside her. She arched herself upward, wanting to be as close as possible to him.

As he thrust inside her, filling her with his essence, she could feel them, from head to foot, mixing themselves within each other. Her hands pressed into his back and shoulders, and instead of feeling firm, muscled flesh, she seemed to move through him and touch his inner soul.

She felt Max nuzzle his head in the crook of her neck, and move right through her until he kissed her very heart. Her chest rose, merged inside his chest.

The short span of time — it could only have been a few minutes at most — seemed to stretch, to last forever. She felt Max in every inch of her flesh, his shaft throbbing inside her, his chest inside hers, his hands running through her body, his head and face kissing her, licking her. And she felt herself reach up inside him to touch and caress as well.

It felt indescribable, so intensely intimate she knew there would never be another for her. And as they drew away, as they came down from their passion, she opened her eyes to find a blue, sparkling glow surrounding them. They were not bathed in the blue light anymore, they *were* the source of blue light.

Kyli found herself drawing in deep, steadying breaths, trying to sort out in her mind the last few minutes. Max didn't remove his cock, but did turn them toward each other, lying side-by-side on the spacious bed.

She looked into his eyes, enjoyed seeing the contrast between his dark skin and her lighter hands caressing him.

"Wow," he said, smiling drowsily, "that will be hard to top."

Kyli laughed softly. "We'll work something out."

Max simply nodded and gently, reverently, touched her skin, the blue and silver collar around her neck.

"Pretty intense, huh? I don't think I'll ever see that necklace and not be able to think of this. Can't wait to get back home and try that one again."

Kyli smiled and hugged him.

"It will only get better with time and exploration," came a soft voice from behind them. Kyli half-turned and saw She'sa behind her, coming towards the bed.

"You should have told me earlier, She," she laughed. "I would have Bonded long before now!"

The Priestess smiled and stopped.

"You weren't ready before now. Neither was your Bondmate."

Kyli felt a tiny moment of loss as Max withdrew himself from her. He sat up and, reluctant to totally lose the intimate, private moment with him, she sat up on the bed as well.

When She'sa held out a hand to her, she took it and was helped from the bed. She saw Max also climb from the bed out of the corner of her eye as her friend hugged her.

"Congratulations, you're now a Bonded woman."

Kyli smiled at her friend, happily accepting the well-wishes from her. A shot of surprise rushed through her as her friend kissed her on the lips.

The kiss was chaste, only a benediction of sorts. A soft press of lips on lips. Kyli felt so mellow, she allowed it. She felt as if a ghostly, spiritual hand passed through her. It felt warm, almost as if someone caressed her, but caressed her *insides* instead of her outer flesh.

Kyli felt a moment of surprise, as she had never kissed a woman before and never had the inclination. Before she could wonder, She'sa had pulled away.

"Blessings on your Bonding, Kyli. It will be long and happy and fruitful."

Kyli laughed as her sense of humor overtook her.

"Vague but promising. How very you, She." Tilting her head, she gazed at her. "You're a good friend, She'sa."

Kyli felt Max come up beside her and move to put an arm around her. Instead, She'sa stepped forward and, cupping his face, also kissed him. Kyli smiled and watched, fascinated. Max had frozen, being taken by surprise.

The kiss was again chaste, a simple pressing of lips on lips. Yet Kyli noticed something wispy seemed to pass between them. She remembered the warm hand that had seemingly passed through her and thought maybe it *was* some sort of benediction from the Priestess.

Seconds later, She'sa had pulled away. Much as Kyli loved her friend, she couldn't help the feminine grin that crossed her face as Max took a step back to her side so he could wrap a large arm around her still naked shoulder. Kyli felt blessed and so happy she could barely believe it.

"I'll miss you, my friend," She'sa said, looking warmly at her. Kyli felt a faint blush creep on her cheeks and tried hard to ignore it. "Please come back, both of you, any time and visit. I would love that."

Kyli grinned. "We'll keep in touch, She, don't worry about it." She looked up to Max as she enjoyed the warmth his arm gave her. He smiled and nodded.

"We'd better get dressed and head on out." Max said, his voice husky with desire she could clearly read in his eyes. "Gregor will be getting impatient."

Kyli laughed and kissed her Bondmate.

"That means we had to get moving. I don't think he'd appreciate a naked comm." Cocking her head, she paused and thought. "Then again, *I* could comm him naked and he wouldn't mind—" she squealed happily as Max grabbed her and lightly slapped her ass.

"No more talking like that, young lady! You're a happily Bonded woman. Bonded women do *not* call other men while naked. Do they, She'sa?"

Kyli broke free from Max's embrace and turned to where her friend had stood.

"She'sa?" she called, her voice echoing in the room. Looking to Max, she shrugged.

"Come on, Kyli. Let's get dressed. Hopefully someone will come by and lead us back to our bags and then help us out of this place."

Laughing, exchanging kisses and caresses, Kyli climbed back into her gown and stockings. The panties she decided to leave until Max took them and placed them in his pocket.

"Souvenir," he winked at her. She laughed and shook her head.

A novice came into the room just as they finished dressing themselves. They were led back to their rooms and collected their belongings, now packed again in their bags. Kyli didn't see She'sa again, but knew her friend was happy for them both.

Holding hands, they exited the temple. Kyli felt shocked to realize only a little over an hour had passed.

"We going to comm Gregor?" she asked as they headed toward the port.

"Not right now, nah. I don't want to give the man more reasons to gripe at me. It must be a truly terrible time over there. I'll message him a little later and we can just visit him when we reach back home."

Kyli laughed. "Do you think he'll be surprised? It's been one hell of a day."

Max stopped still in the middle of the street. The other pedestrians behind them cursed as they wrapped each other in a tight embrace. Max bent his head and kissed her, long and deep.

Minutes later, Kyli raised her head, breathless.

"I think old Gregor will be pleased and proud of us. Jealous as hell, but pleased and proud."

Kyli smiled, stared into the dark brown eyes of her love.

"Thank you for making all my fantasies come true, Max. Not just the threesome, but all of them."

"Baby," he whispered, nuzzling under her ear, "I haven't even begun yet. We still have those clamps to play with, the mammary orgasms, a whole plethora of fantasy stuff we haven't even begun on. But personally, I like the anal scenes best. I can't wait for 'Barbarian takes the Virgin Priestess'."

Kyli laughed lightly, pulling away. "Well then, let's head on out. I think we should go on a Bonded trip for a few days, do a bit of physical exploring."

Kyli sent a naughty glance to Max under her lashes.

"Personally, I'm thinking a bit of private time between the two of us before we head home would be a good thing. We both have the time and you should have some leave due to you, what more perfect time to…explore?"

Max stared at her as she ran a hand seductively over the top of her chest.

"Hmm…" he said noncommittally, so she really put on the heat.

"I'm rather eager to try out some of those fantasy scenes myself," Kyli said seductively, stretching her body enticingly, "and just think of all the new ones we can think up and write down."

She laughed as Max just looked at her. She knew him well enough now to know the small tick in his jaw meant he wanted to do naughty things with her and to her. When he wrapped one arm around her shoulder and began to lead them once more to the Port, she laughed aloud.

"Oh come on! You can't possibly expect me to not believe you want to spend a few days just cruising around the stars, running around and playing?"

When Max grunted, she smiled to herself, knowing she had won the war. They would take some time out, just for the two of them together.

Slowly, they headed down the street, taking their time. Max lowered his arm, so they easily, gently held hands. As the streets passed, Kyli caught her breath and covered her mouth as she yawned, "Or maybe we can play around after I take a short nap. I didn't realize quite how late it really was."

"I think we can indulge in a bit of sleep," Max said easily, leaning forward teasingly to her. Kyli laughed and swatted him with her spare hand, which he then grabbed and held hostage in one of his large hands.

"I think I'll have to make some more fantasies that involve restraining you and letting me have my wicked way with you. 'Priestess and the Slave Boy' sounds good to me at this point in time."

Max simply grinned and raised an eyebrow. He didn't even need to say the words, she could practically read his mind.

She sighed dramatically.

"Okay, you can also have a few 'Space Pirate and the Virgin Novice' scenarios as well. But you'd better make it worth my while, buddy!"

Kyli felt her breath catch as Max stopped them both and gently, softly laid a kiss on her lips. He pulled back slowly, letting their bodies touch at every point.

"Don't you worry, baby. It would be my pleasure."

# Epilogue
*Gregor's residence*

Gregor pulled his mind out of the foggy encryption-filled buzz in his head. He had no idea how long the message-received light on his PCC had been flashing. When he entered deeply into his mind to play with some code, he often forgot everything in the whole galaxy and could only focus on his thoughts.

He pulled up the message and smiled at the comm Max had sent him.

*Sorry mate, no more threesomes for us. Bonded bliss is a zillion times better than they say. Dirty trick btw, that whole bottle bomb thing was brilliant. Remind me to break your neck next time I see you. Don't comm for a few days, we'll be busy. Max and Kyli.*

Gregor truly felt happy for his two friends, but instead of turning straight back to his encryption, as he would have expected of himself, he looked out his window at the mid-afternoon sun. A couple of minutes ticked by and Gregor tried to put his finger on the strange thoughts and feelings swirling through his body.

With quite a shock, he realized he felt slightly jealous of Max. Gregor didn't kid himself and think that without Kyli being a sexual buddy his life would be blighted, but he did feel unsettled at his two best friends Bonding and settling down like the proverbial couple.

Even his "jealousy" wasn't the fiery, tempestuous heat it should have been had he truly loved Kyli in a deeply forever manner. For all of five minutes, he tried to feel anything other than a vague kind of warmth, which wasn't exactly happiness nor exactly a real sense of jealousy for his two friends.

Gregor knew in his deepest heart he had acknowledged many years ago that those two were perfect for each other. Gregor also had to admit to himself he had purposely set out to reunite both Max and Kyli, although even he hadn't dared hope for so much to spark between them so quickly.

After he and Max had renewed their friendship and Gregor had learned his old friend still lusted after Kyli, Gregor had decided it certainly couldn't hurt to experiment between the three of them. Once he had made the initial decision, very little digging needed to be done to discover Kyli had put herself in line for a termination of her merc contracts. Unearthing her application to the Force had been so easy he could have done it in his sleep.

Carefully setting up his conversations with Max, reminiscing about their wet team days, drawing him out slowly, Gregor had brought Max to the decision to meet back up with his old flame.

Subtly, Gregor had oh-so-casually dropped into the conversation Kyli's old fantasy of having a threesome. Teasing and tempting Max into making that fantasy a reality for the three of them had been child's play.

Disentangling himself had been harder, Gregor silently acknowledged, but still a challenge he had enjoyed. The overall challenge of setting Max and Kyli up, with neither of them noticing or understanding had truly been one of his best ideas ever.

Gregor stood up and crossed over to his secondary desktop computer. He opened up a couple of files and began to type up the encryption his life had become. Gregor wondered for a moment if his dissatisfaction with life in general might have something to do with the fact he hadn't had something new to keep his mind active in a very long time.

Encryptions had been his life for almost as long as he could remember, they had always been enough to keep him active and interested in the world around him. Yet working with Max for so long, and the immeasurable way his life had deepened and felt richer for his interactions with Max and Kyli, had made him wonder a few things.

Gregor opened up the flow charts and began to insert all the relevant data from his recent experiences. He drew up the encryption flow plans of how his life had progressed, with special emphasis on the last few days.

As the greater picture began to emerge, Gregor acknowledged to himself he needed something extra to put some spark back in his life, something his interactions with Max and Kyli had begun but not been enough for. Gregor went into more details, went over the new encryptions he had entered and fleshed out more details. The more he added, the more he typed and the deeper he dug into his own psyche, the better he understood just how lonely and completely isolated he had been from everyone and everything in recent years.

Frowning, Gregor typed even more. It wasn't as if he never got laid. Frowning even deeper, he leaned over and typed back through his calendar. *Four months?* He could hardly believe it! The last woman he had slept with before his night with Kyli had been *four months* ago?

Incredulous, he slowly scanned through the dates and meetings in his personal calendar. It had to have been that long at the very least, he realized with shock. And he could only vaguely remember the woman whom he had let drag him back to her hotel room. Marthe? Had that been her name? Maybe it had been Marzina?

Gregor cast her from his mind, he certainly couldn't picture her, and although he did feel slightly guilty over not remembering her name, he had only let her pick him up from a bon voyage party they had both been attending.

He might need to get laid, but he didn't truly think that was the main problem. It was his lack of emotional attachment to any of the women he knew. *That's what I'm missing,* he thought as he typed more furiously on his machine, *it's the emotional connection. I have a personal, integral understanding with both Max and Kyli, our friendship give a deeper meaning to our interactions.*

Gregor continued to type his accepted thoughts into the flow chart. The creation emerging felt like a massive revelation. By immersing himself in his work, by limiting his interactions to only people who understood his encryptions and resources, he had lost the integral personal connection all living beings needed.

Getting laid might help him physically, but it wouldn't solve the deeper problem he felt himself coming to understand. The more his understanding of the situation grew, the deeper his worry over the problem he faced became.

He needed a woman who could be a friend and a confidant to him. He needed to find a woman who was a challenge as well as an enigma to keep his mind active, but one who understood him and his mind well enough to accept his total package. Sometimes when he buried himself in a problem, he mightn't emerge for hours at a time, what sort of woman would put up with that?

The sheer enormity of what he unearthed made him dizzy for a moment. His restlessness and odd feelings over Max and Kyli finding such wonderful, Bonded bliss together had unearthed his own desires for such a close connection to a woman.

For a moment, he stared outside his window in sheer terror. Since when had he wanted to share the depths of his soul with another person, let alone a woman who would never fully understand him?

He needed to be in control of his life, he needed to have a deep, fully accepting sexual relationship. Most women could barely keep up with his needs and sexual demands for one night. How the five hells was he supposed to find a women rare enough to want it forever?

Gregor shook his head.

He must be mistaken. Maybe there was a glitch in his flow plans code or something. He had never needed a woman like that, as a friend, companion as well as a lover, and so he surely didn't need one now. He just needed a new challenge at work, that was all. Gregor nodded to himself and stood up from his desk.

Walking back across to his work console, he tried to shake all his strange, completely alien thoughts from his mind. He would re-run the encryptions and data later on, maybe another day. He felt certain a new project at work would do the trick since he didn't need a woman to share his life with.

Everything had been growing increasingly dull at work since he had stopped going out on the more hands-on missions. Maybe it was the excitement factor he was missing, the lack of physical dangers in his work.

*Yeah,* he thought to himself, *that's it, no more adrenalin and endorphin rushes is making me wish for hearth and home and the perfect little woman to warm my bed and cook my meals. Must be that.*

Gregor sat back at his console and began to get back to work. Maybe he should ask to re-assign himself at work, or maybe he should take up some of the more dangerous tips he and Max had decided not to follow through on with their investigations firm.

*Perfect,* he patted himself mentally on the back. *I'll head out for parts unknown and follow through some of the more dangerous things, that will work a treat.*

Smiling, sinking back into his encryptions, Gregor felt his heart beat a fast tattoo against his chest as his mind flashed with a vision of a woman. Deep, soulful blue eyes crossed his mind for a split second, until he regained his wits enough to shake them away forcefully before the rest of the beautiful face could fully form.

He didn't need a woman. He had only begun to think he might because Max was so obscenely happy with Kyli. He needed more excitement, more daring adventures and tales of derring-do to fulfill his life. He would comm Max after he and Kyli had finished their extended leave and then he could head back out into the galaxy, fighting the good fight.

He would get his head back into all the danger and adventure and obliterate all thoughts of settling down. He wasn't that sort of life anyway. He was a loner, a one-night-stand man. Women always complained that he wanted too much, asked for more than they could give.

Gregor forced all the thoughts out of his head and settled down in front of his holo-screen. Re-reading over the last few commands he had planted, he let his mind tick over once more with the complex series of symbols and patterns.

If he managed to crack the few remaining problems here, he could possibly finish this program and ask for a new project before Max returned. A new project would help keep his mind busy until they could decide which new investigation to begin, and then he could go back out into the field.

Smiling happily, Gregor set about the final tweaking on his next encryption program. Tapping happily, he lost himself once more in his own world, never knowing what the future might bring, but certain he could deal with anything the goddess decided to throw at him.

## About the author:

Elizabeth Lapthorne is the eldest of four children. She grew up with lots of noise, fights and tale-telling. Her mother, a reporter and book reviewer, instilled in her a great appreciation of reading with the intrigues of a good plot.

Elizabeth studied Science at school, and whilst between jobs complained bitterly to a good friend about the lack of current literature to pass away the hours. While they both were looking up websites for new publishers, she stumbled onto Ellora's Cave. Jumping head-first into this doubly new site (both the first e-book site she had ever visited, as well as her first taste of Romantica) they both devoured over half of EC's titles in less than a month. While waiting for more titles to be printed (as well as that ever-elusive science job) Elizabeth started dabbling again in her writing.

Elizabeth has always loved to read, it will always be her favourite pass-time, (she is constantly buying new books and bookshelves to fill), but she also loves going to the beach, sitting in the sun, having coffee (or better yet, CHOCOLATE and coffee) with her friends and generally enjoying life. She is extremely curious, which is why she studied science, and often tells "interesting" stories, loving a good laugh. She is a self-confessed email junkie, loving to read what other people on the EC board think and have to say, she laughs often at their tales and ideas. She recently has developed a taste for the gym. She's sure she read somewhere it was good for her, but she is reserving judgment to see how long it lasts.

Elizabeth welcomes mail from readers. You can write to her c/o Ellora's Cave Publishing at 1056 Home Avenue, Akron OH 44310-3502.

# Why an electronic book?

We live in the Information Age—an exciting time in the history of human civilization in which technology rules supreme and continues to progress in leaps and bounds every minute of every hour of every day. For a multitude of reasons, more and more avid literary fans are opting to purchase e-books instead of paperbacks. The question to those not yet initiated to the world of electronic reading is simply: *why?*

1. *Price.* An electronic title at Ellora's Cave Publishing and Cerridwen Press runs anywhere from 40-75% less than the cover price of the <u>exact same title</u> in paperback format. Why? Cold mathematics. It is less expensive to publish an e-book than it is to publish a paperback, so the savings are passed along to the consumer.

2. *Space.* Running out of room to house your paperback books? That is one worry you will never have with electronic novels. For a low one-time cost, you can purchase a handheld computer designed specifically for e-reading purposes. Many e-readers are larger than the average handheld, giving you plenty of screen room. Better yet, hundreds of titles can be stored within your new library—a single microchip. (Please note that Ellora's Cave and Cerridwen Press does not endorse any specific brands. You can check our website at www.ellorascave.com or

www.cerridwenpress.com for customer recommendations we make available to new consumers.)

3. *Mobility.* Because your new library now consists of only a microchip, your entire cache of books can be taken with you wherever you go.

4. *Personal preferences are accounted for.* Are the words you are currently reading too small? Too large? Too...**ANNOYING**? Paperback books cannot be modified according to personal preferences, but e-books can.

5. *Instant gratification.* Is it the middle of the night and all the bookstores are closed? Are you tired of waiting days—sometimes weeks—for online and offline bookstores to ship the novels you bought? Ellora's Cave Publishing sells instantaneous downloads 24 hours a day, 7 days a week, 365 days a year. Our e-book delivery system is 100% automated, meaning your order is filled as soon as you pay for it.

Those are a few of the top reasons why electronic novels are displacing paperbacks for many an avid reader. As always, Ellora's Cave and Cerridwen Press welcomes your questions and comments. We invite you to email us at service@ellorascave.com, service@cerridwenpress.com or write to us directly at: 1056 Home Ave. Akron OH 44310-3502.